My Little Pony

Adventures in Friendship

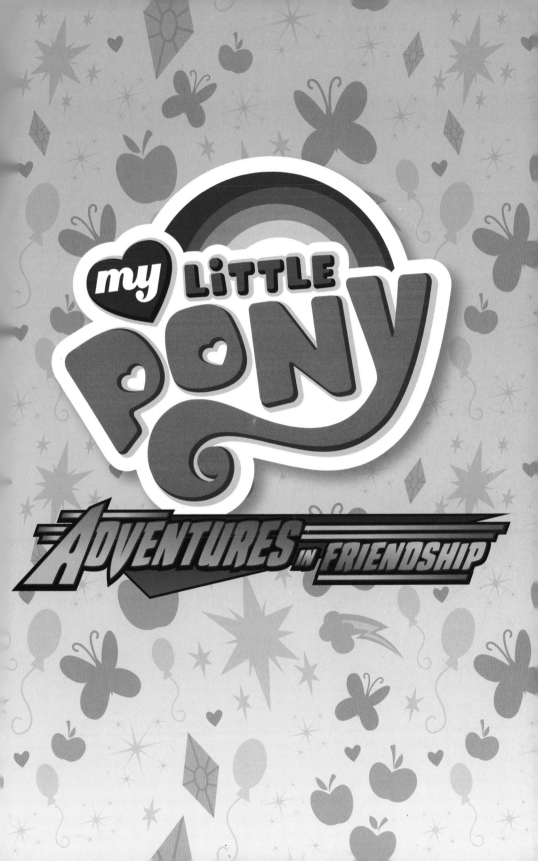

HC COVER BY **SARA RICHARD**
TPB COVER BY **THOM ZAHLER**

COLLECTION EDITS BY **JUSTIN EISINGER** AND **ALONZO SIMON**
COLLECTION DESIGN BY **THOM ZAHLER**

Special thanks to Erin Comella, Robert Fewkes, Joe Furfaro, Heather Hopkins, Pat Jarret, Ed Lane, Brian Lenard, Marissa Mansolillo, Donna Tobin, Michael Vogel, and Michael Kelly for their invaluable assistance.

HC ISBN: 978-1-63140-360-6 • TPB ISBN: 978-1-63140-428-3   18 17 16 15   1 2 3 4

IDW
® Licensed By: Hasbro

www.IDWPUBLISHING.com
IDW founded by Ted Adams, Alex Garner, Kris Oprisko, and Robbie Robbins

Ted Adams, CEO & Publisher
Greg Goldstein, President & COO
Robbie Robbins, EVP/Sr. Graphic Artist
Chris Ryall, Chief Creative Officer/Editor-in-Chief
Matthew Ruzicka, CPA, Chief Financial Officer
Alan Payne, VP of Sales
Dirk Wood, VP of Marketing
Lorelei Bunjes, VP of Digital Services
Jeff Webber, VP of Digital Publishing & Business Development

Facebook: **facebook.com/idwpublishing**
Twitter: **@idwpublishing**
YouTube: **youtube.com/idwpublishing**
Instagram: **instagram.com/idwpublishing**
deviantART: **idwpublishing.deviantart.com**
Pinterest: **pinterest.com/idwpublishing/idw-staff-faves**

Originally published as MY LITTLE PONY MICRO-SERIES #8: PRINCESS CELESTIA, MY LITTLE PONY MICRO-SERIES #9: SPIKE, and MY LITTLE PONY: FRIENDS FOREVER #3.

CHAPTER ONE
PRINCESS CELESTIA

WRITTEN BY **GEORGIA BALL**
ART BY **AMY MEBBERSON**
LETTERS BY **NEIL UYETAKE**

CHAPTER TWO

SPIKE

WRITTEN BY **ROB ANDERSON**
ART BY **AGNES GARBOWSKA**
LETTERS BY **NEIL UYETAKE**

CHAPTER THREE

PRINCESS CELESTIA AND SPIKE

WRITTEN BY **TED ANDERSON**
ART BY **AGNES GARBOWSKA**
LETTERS BY **NEIL UYETAKE**

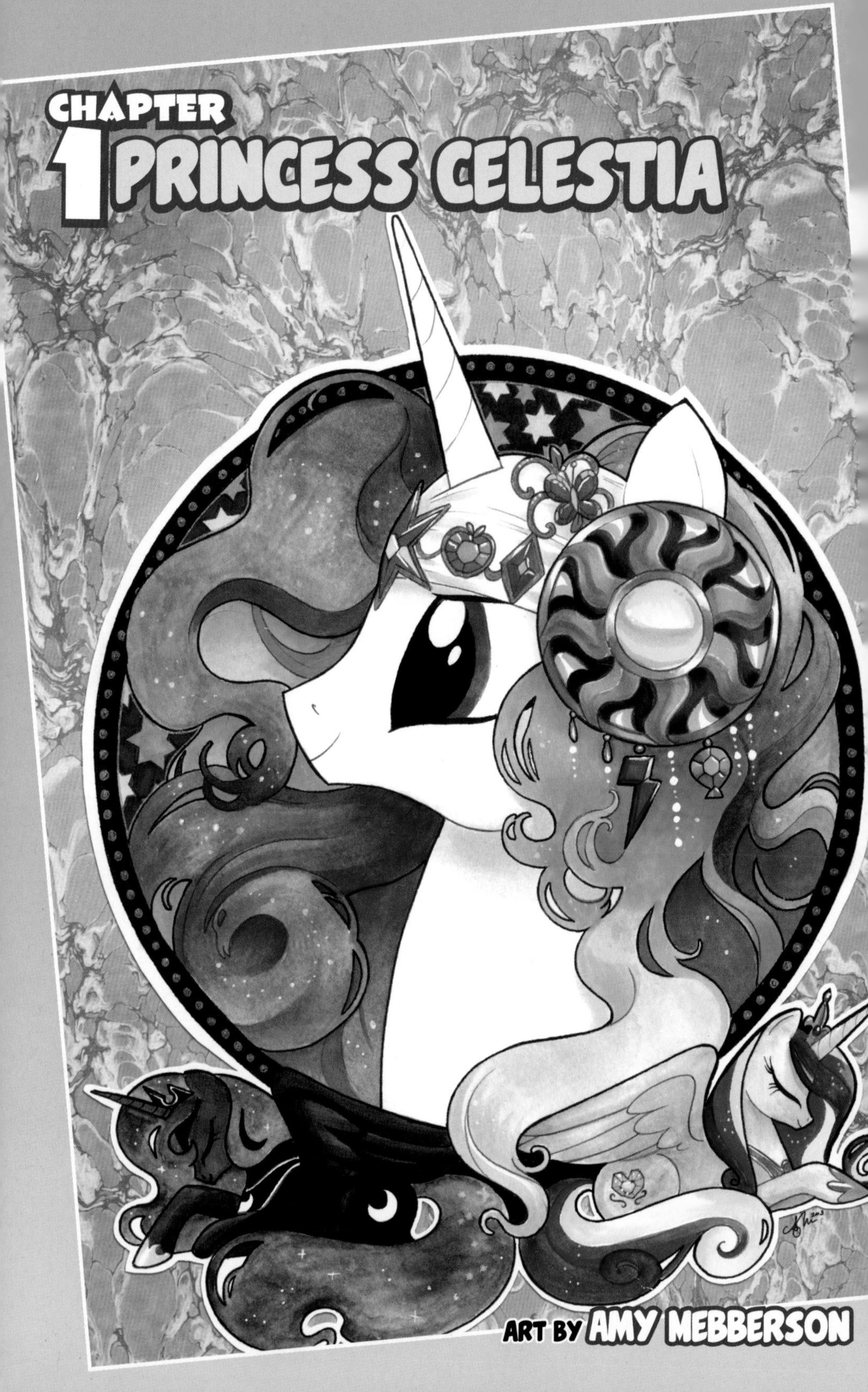
CHAPTER 1 PRINCESS CELESTIA
ART BY AMY MEBBERSON

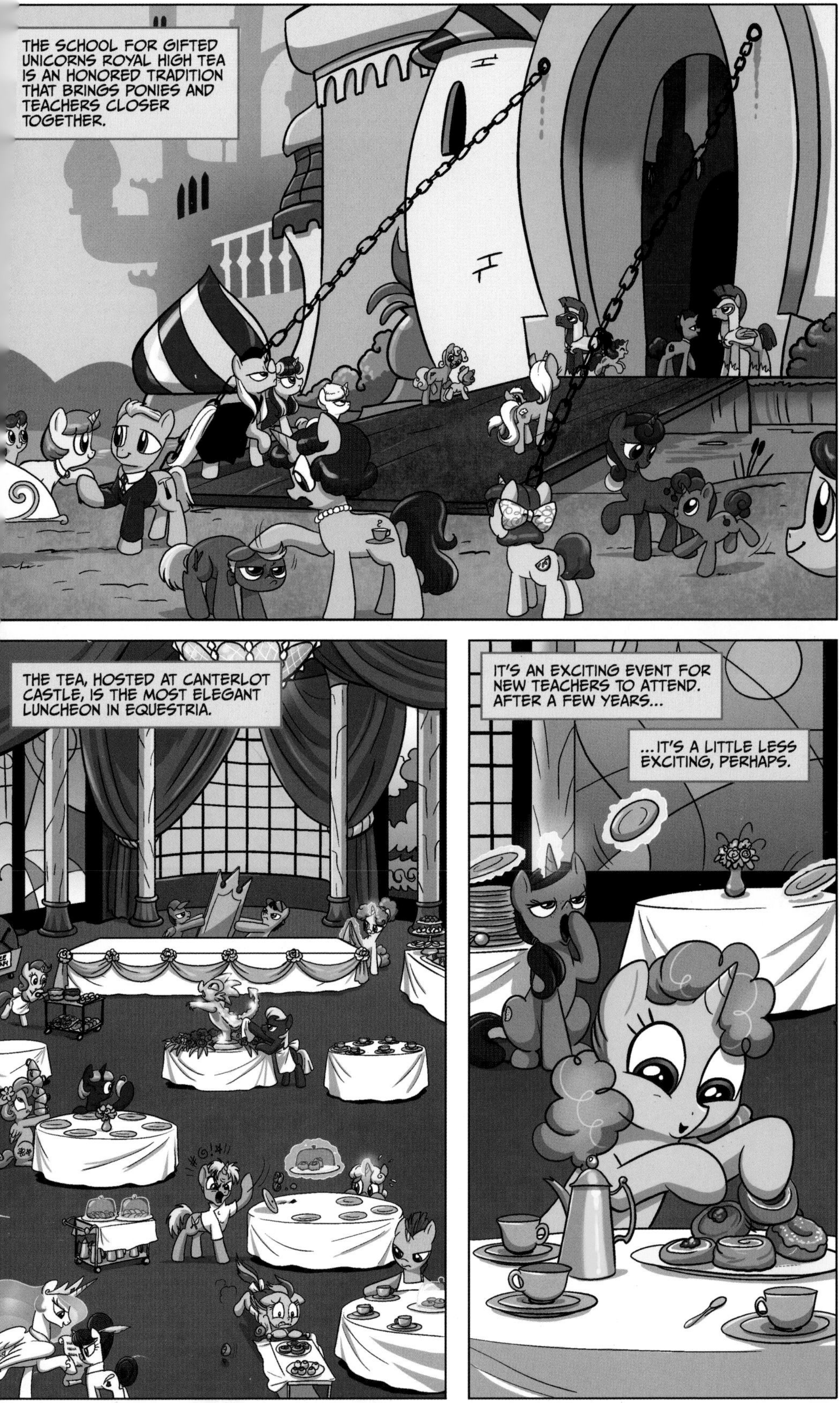
THE SCHOOL FOR GIFTED UNICORNS ROYAL HIGH TEA IS AN HONORED TRADITION THAT BRINGS PONIES AND TEACHERS CLOSER TOGETHER.
THE TEA, HOSTED AT CANTERLOT CASTLE, IS THE MOST ELEGANT LUNCHEON IN EQUESTRIA.
IT'S AN EXCITING EVENT FOR NEW TEACHERS TO ATTEND. AFTER A FEW YEARS...
...IT'S A LITTLE LESS EXCITING, PERHAPS.

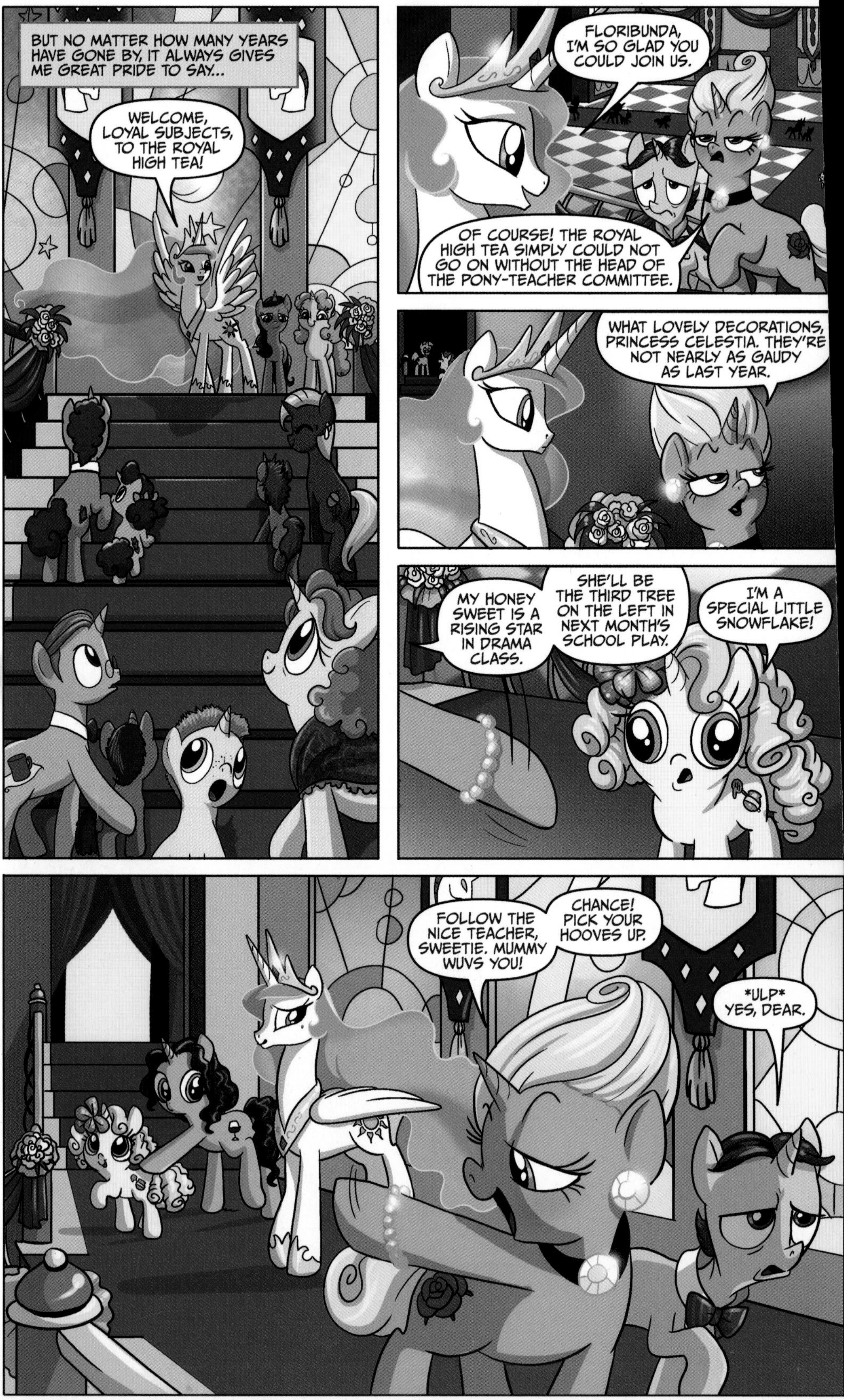
BUT NO MATTER HOW MANY YEARS HAVE GONE BY, IT ALWAYS GIVES ME GREAT PRIDE TO SAY...
WELCOME, LOYAL SUBJECTS, TO THE ROYAL HIGH TEA!
FLORIBUNDA, I'M SO GLAD YOU COULD JOIN US.
OF COURSE! THE ROYAL HIGH TEA SIMPLY COULD NOT GO ON WITHOUT THE HEAD OF THE PONY-TEACHER COMMITTEE.
WHAT LOVELY DECORATIONS, PRINCESS CELESTIA. THEY'RE NOT NEARLY AS GAUDY AS LAST YEAR.
MY HONEY SWEET IS A RISING STAR IN DRAMA CLASS.
SHE'LL BE THE THIRD TREE ON THE LEFT IN NEXT MONTH'S SCHOOL PLAY.
I'M A SPECIAL LITTLE SNOWFLAKE!
FOLLOW THE NICE TEACHER, SWEETIE. MUMMY WUVS YOU!
CHANCE! PICK YOUR HOOVES UP.
ULP YES, DEAR.

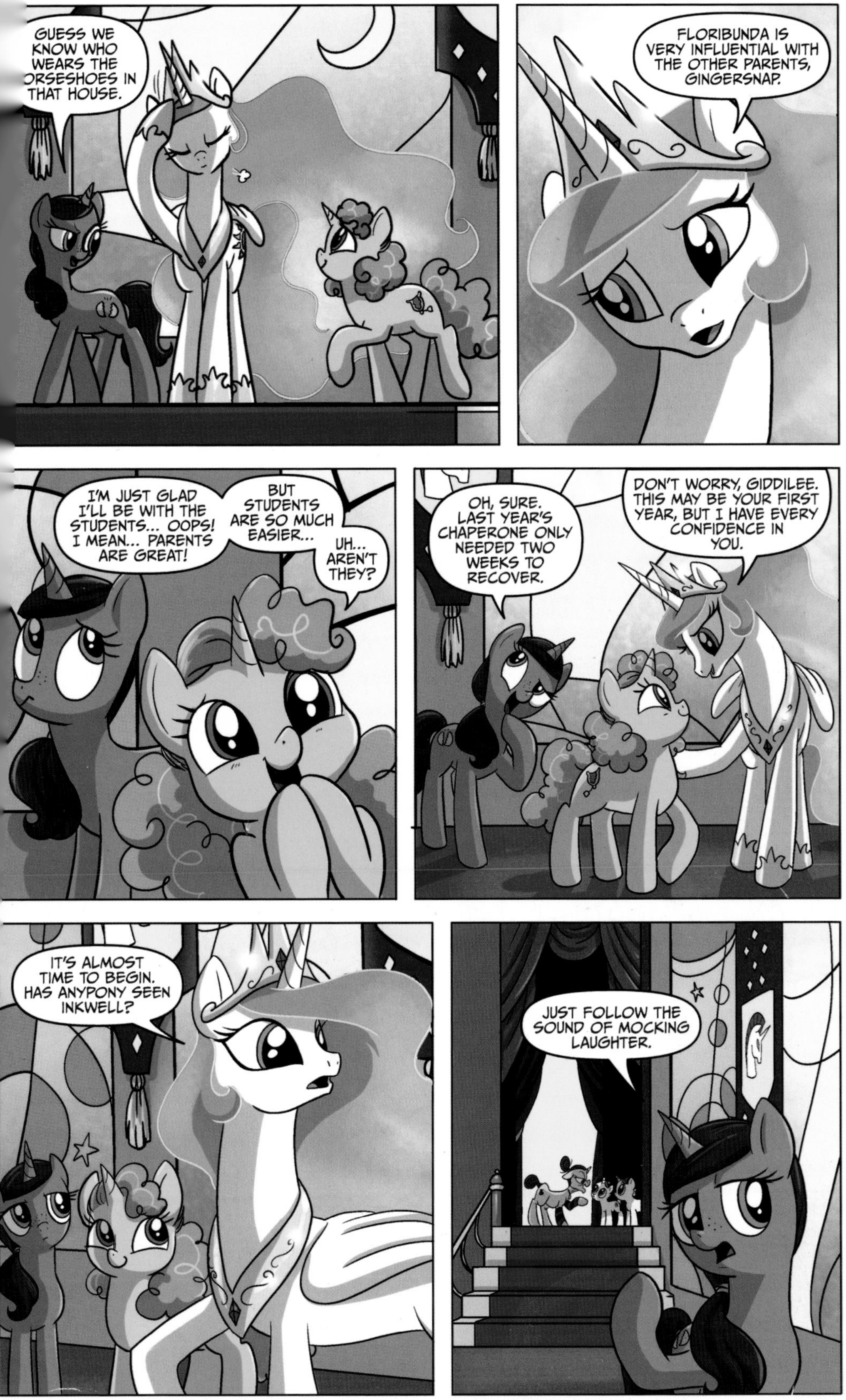
GUESS WE KNOW WHO WEARS THE ORSESHOES IN THAT HOUSE.
FLORIBUNDA IS VERY INFLUENTIAL WITH THE OTHER PARENTS, GINGERSNAP.
I'M JUST GLAD I'LL BE WITH THE STUDENTS... OOPS! I MEAN... PARENTS ARE GREAT!
BUT STUDENTS ARE SO MUCH EASIER...
UH... AREN'T THEY?
OH, SURE. LAST YEAR'S CHAPERONE ONLY NEEDED TWO WEEKS TO RECOVER.
DON'T WORRY, GIDDILEE. THIS MAY BE YOUR FIRST YEAR, BUT I HAVE EVERY CONFIDENCE IN YOU.
IT'S ALMOST TIME TO BEGIN. HAS ANYPONY SEEN INKWELL?
JUST FOLLOW THE SOUND OF MOCKING LAUGHTER.

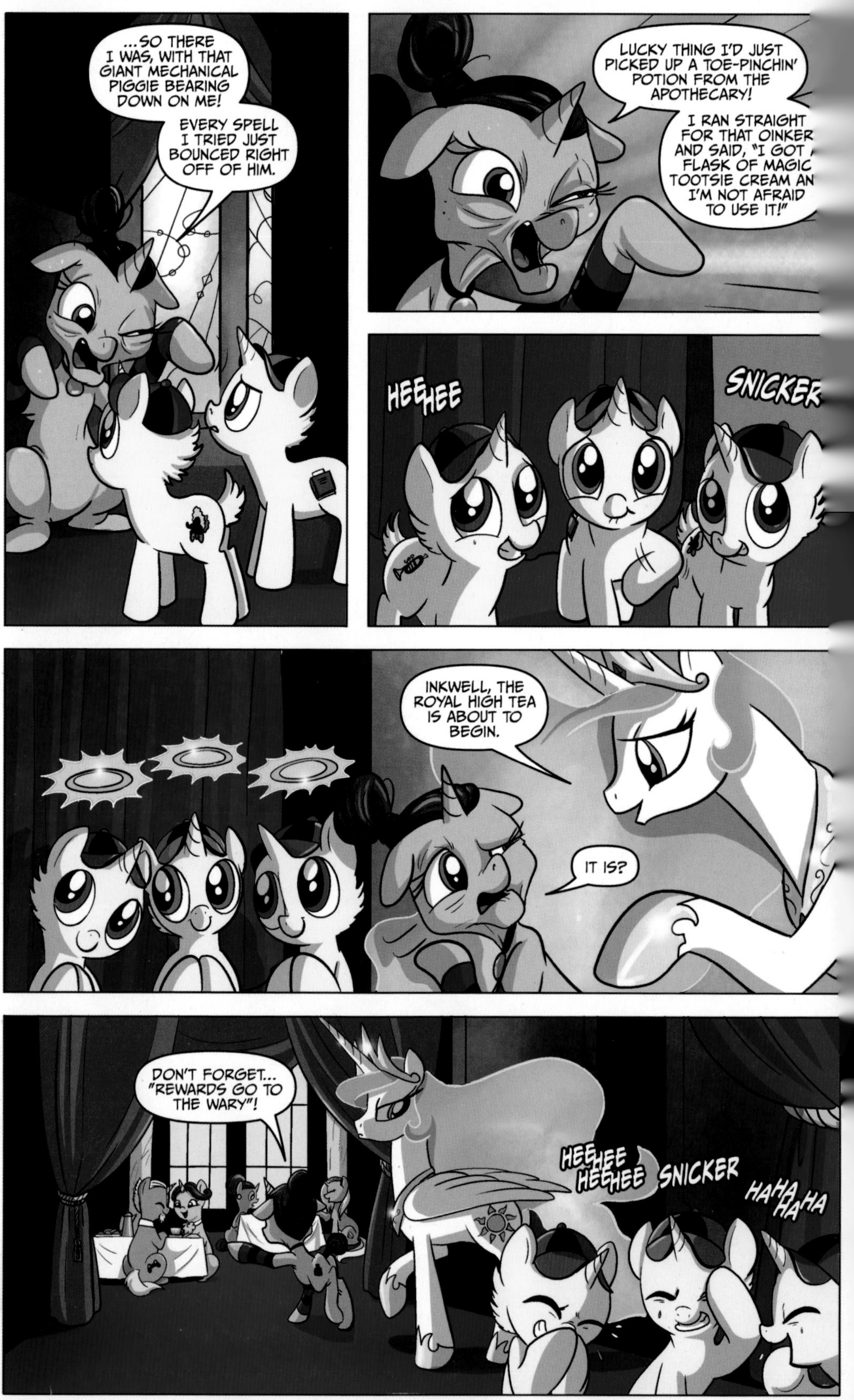
...SO THERE I WAS, WITH THAT GIANT MECHANICAL PIGGIE BEARING DOWN ON ME!
EVERY SPELL I TRIED JUST BOUNCED RIGHT OFF OF HIM.
LUCKY THING I'D JUST PICKED UP A TOE-PINCHIN' POTION FROM THE APOTHECARY!
I RAN STRAIGHT FOR THAT OINKER AND SAID, "I GOT A FLASK OF MAGIC TOOTSIE CREAM AN' I'M NOT AFRAID TO USE IT!"
HEE HEE
SNICKER
INKWELL, THE ROYAL HIGH TEA IS ABOUT TO BEGIN.
IT IS?
DON'T FORGET... "REWARDS GO TO THE WARY"!
HEE HEE HEE HEE
SNICKER
HA HA HA HA

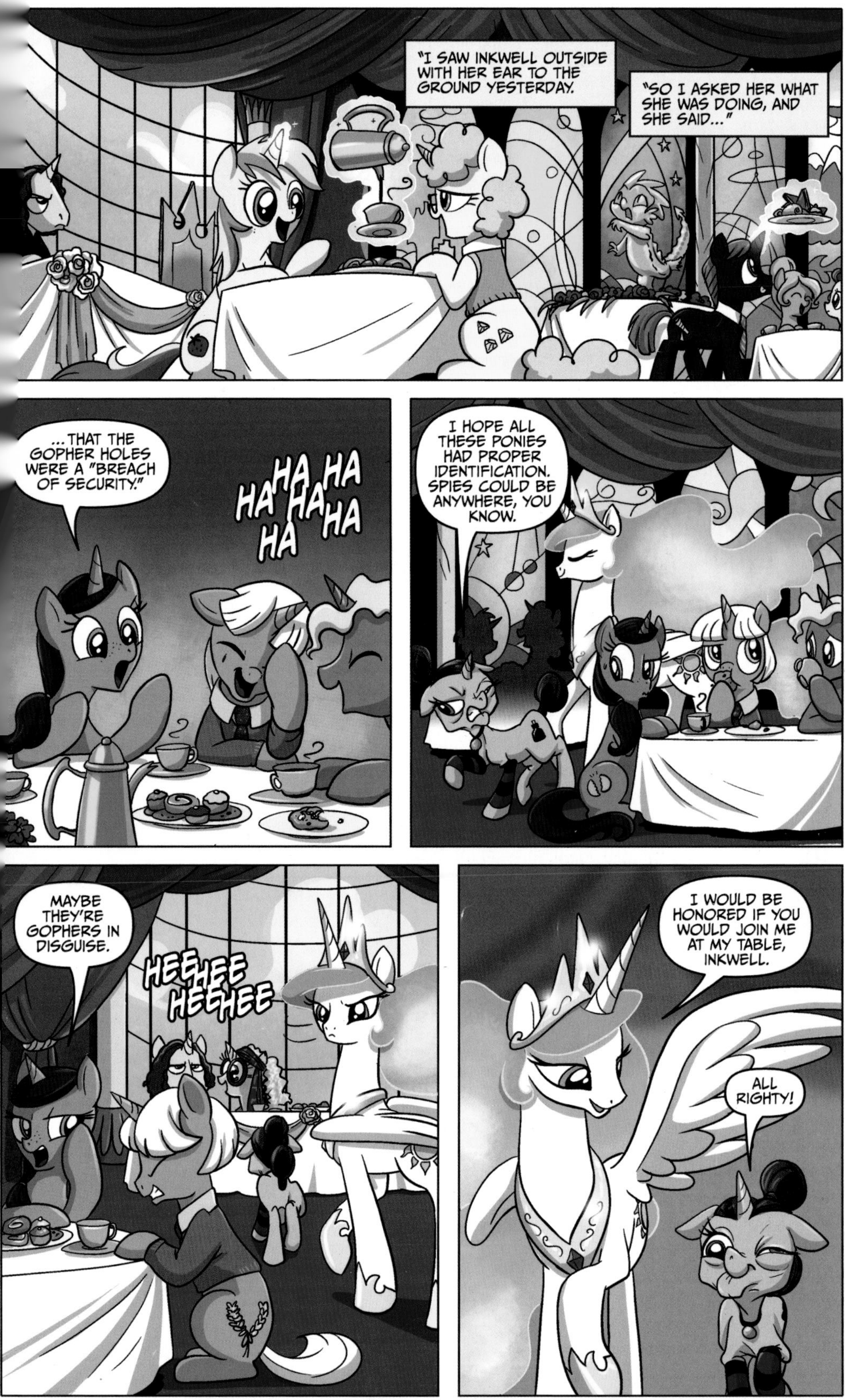
"I SAW INKWELL OUTSIDE WITH HER EAR TO THE GROUND YESTERDAY.
"SO I ASKED HER WHAT SHE WAS DOING, AND SHE SAID..."
...THAT THE GOPHER HOLES WERE A "BREACH OF SECURITY."
HA HA HA HA HA HA HA
I HOPE ALL THESE PONIES HAD PROPER IDENTIFICATION. SPIES COULD BE ANYWHERE, YOU KNOW.
MAYBE THEY'RE GOPHERS IN DISGUISE.
HEE HEE HEE HEE
I WOULD BE HONORED IF YOU WOULD JOIN ME AT MY TABLE, INKWELL.
ALL RIGHTY!

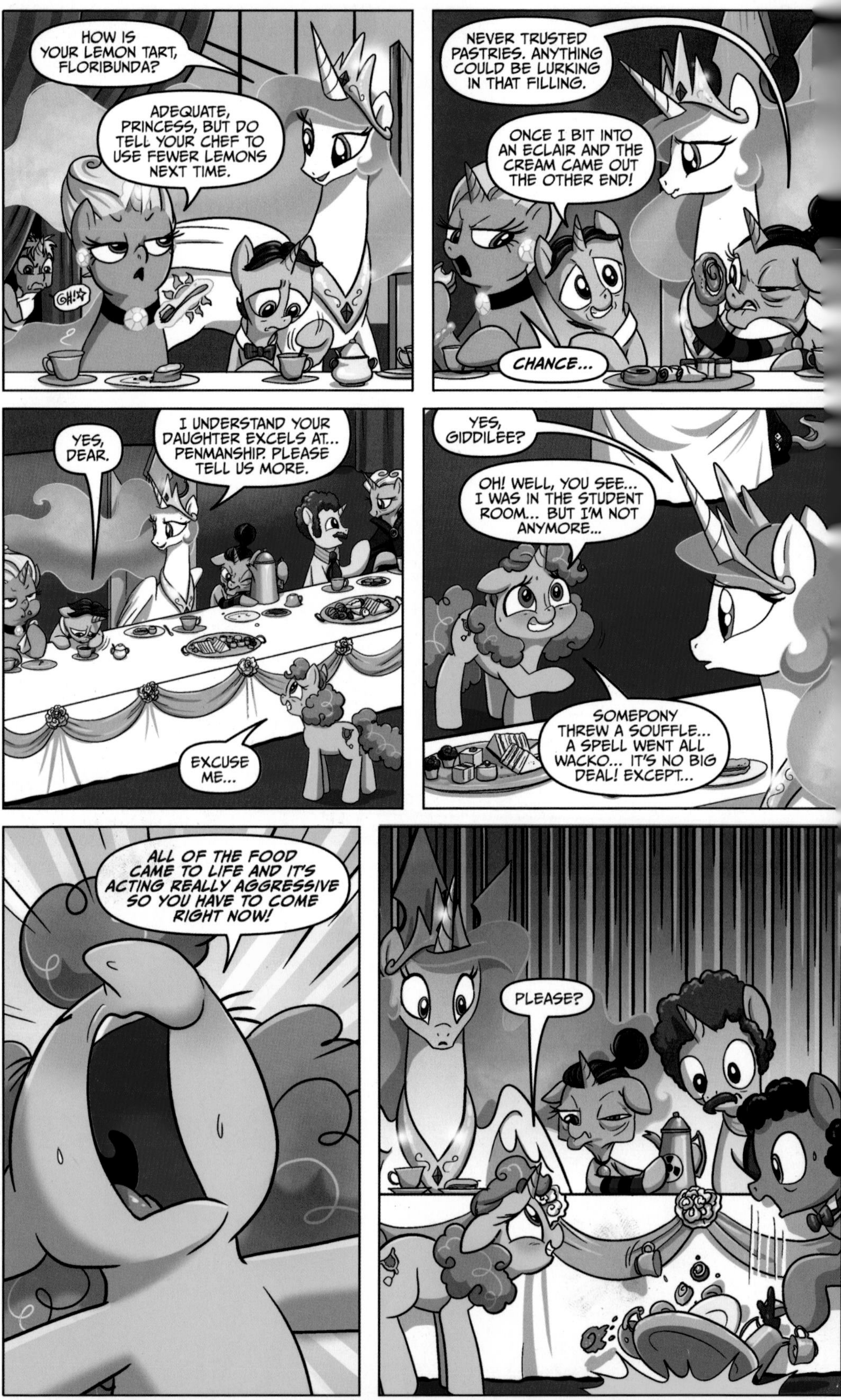
HOW IS YOUR LEMON TART, FLORIBUNDA?
ADEQUATE, PRINCESS, BUT DO TELL YOUR CHEF TO USE FEWER LEMONS NEXT TIME.
GH!☆
NEVER TRUSTED PASTRIES. ANYTHING COULD BE LURKING IN THAT FILLING.
ONCE I BIT INTO AN ECLAIR AND THE CREAM CAME OUT THE OTHER END!
CHANCE...
YES, DEAR.
I UNDERSTAND YOUR DAUGHTER EXCELS AT... PENMANSHIP. PLEASE TELL US MORE.
EXCUSE ME...
YES, GIDDILEE?
OH! WELL, YOU SEE... I WAS IN THE STUDENT ROOM... BUT I'M NOT ANYMORE...
SOMEPONY THREW A SOUFFLE... A SPELL WENT ALL WACKO... IT'S NO BIG DEAL! EXCEPT...
ALL OF THE FOOD CAME TO LIFE AND IT'S ACTING REALLY AGGRESSIVE SO YOU HAVE TO COME RIGHT NOW!
PLEASE?

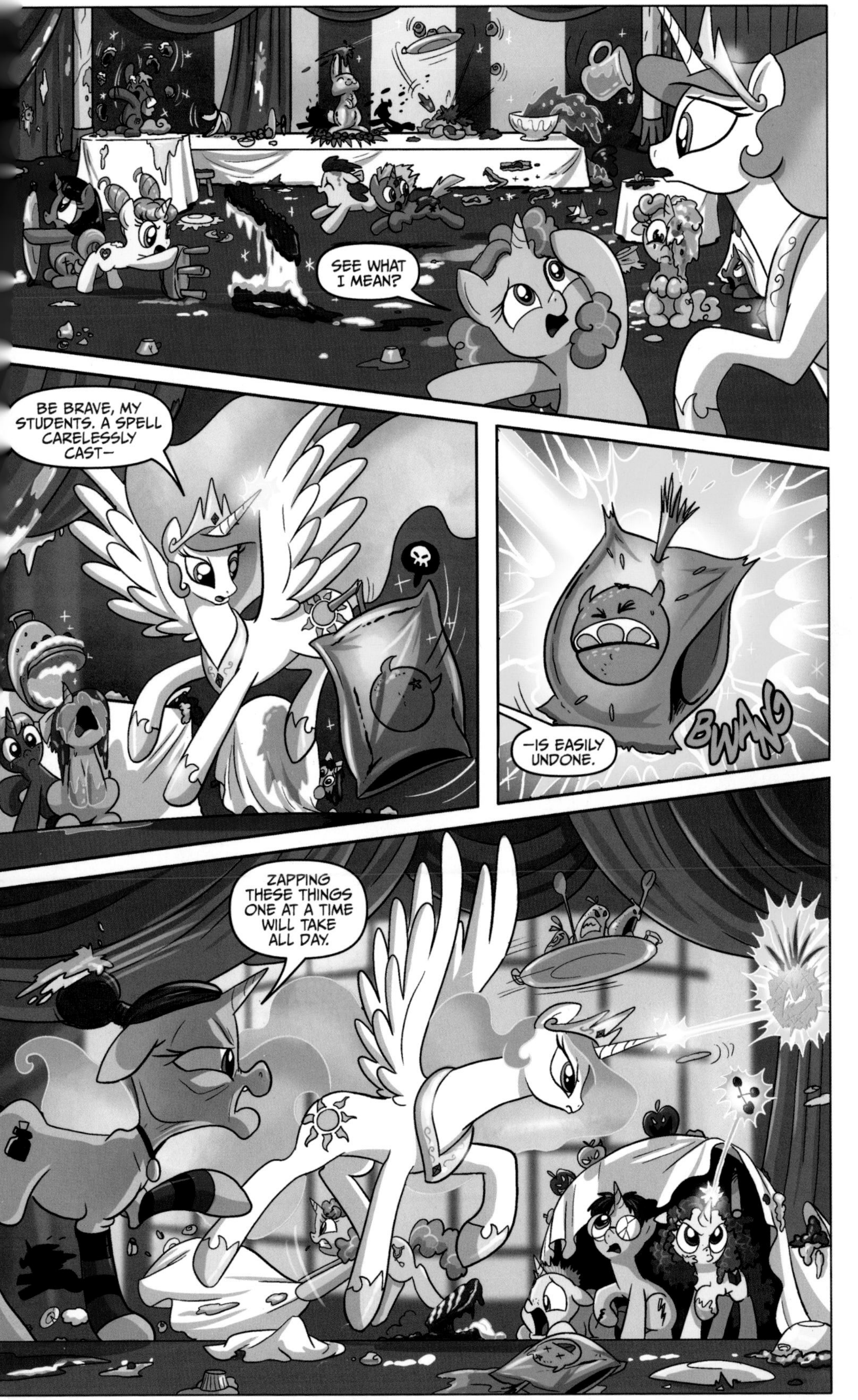
SEE WHAT I MEAN?
BE BRAVE, MY STUDENTS. A SPELL CARELESSLY CAST—
—IS EASILY UNDONE.
BWANG
ZAPPING THESE THINGS ONE AT A TIME WILL TAKE ALL DAY.

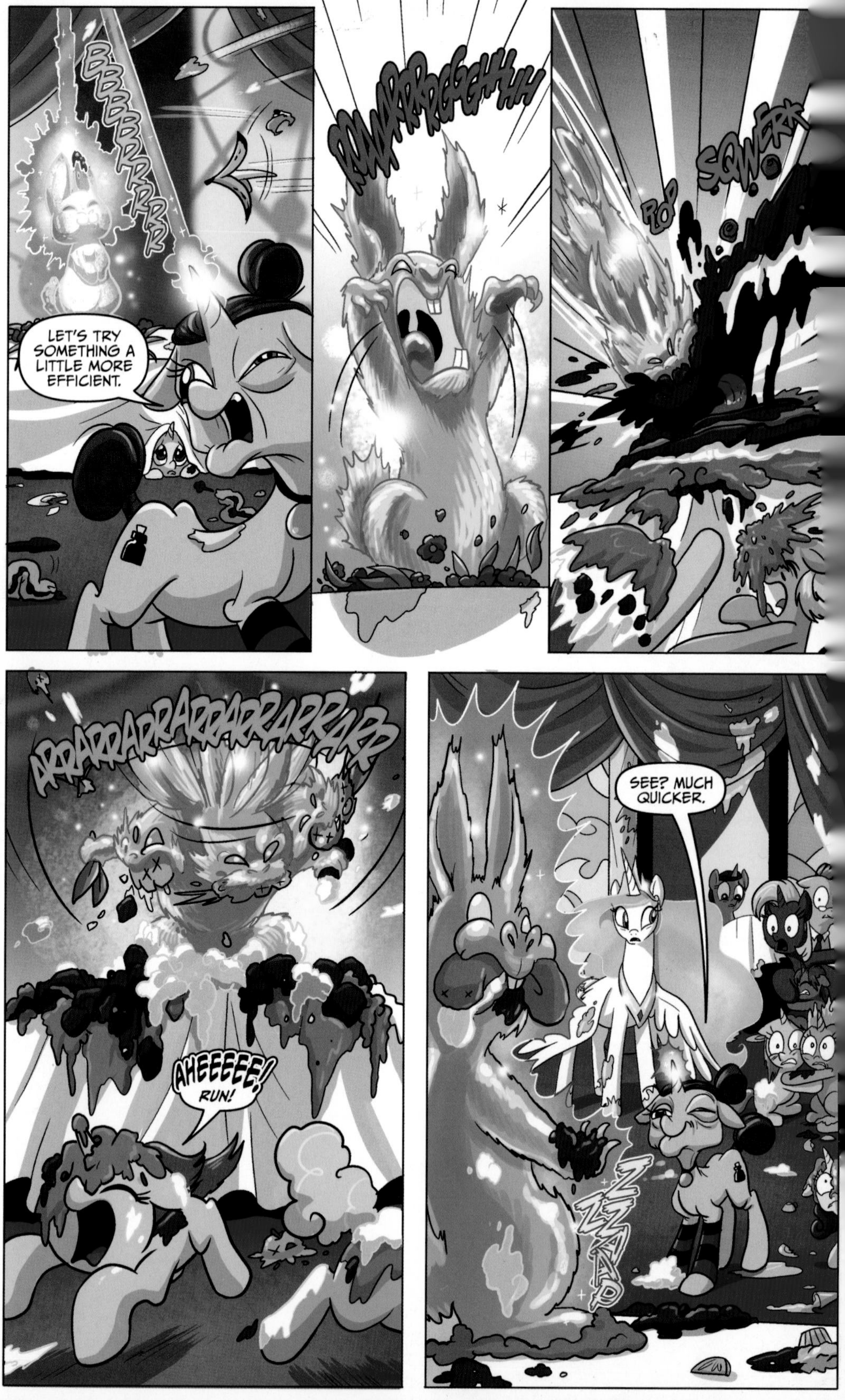
LET'S TRY SOMETHING A LITTLE MORE EFFICIENT.
SQWERK
AHEEEEEE!
RUN!
SEE? MUCH QUICKER.

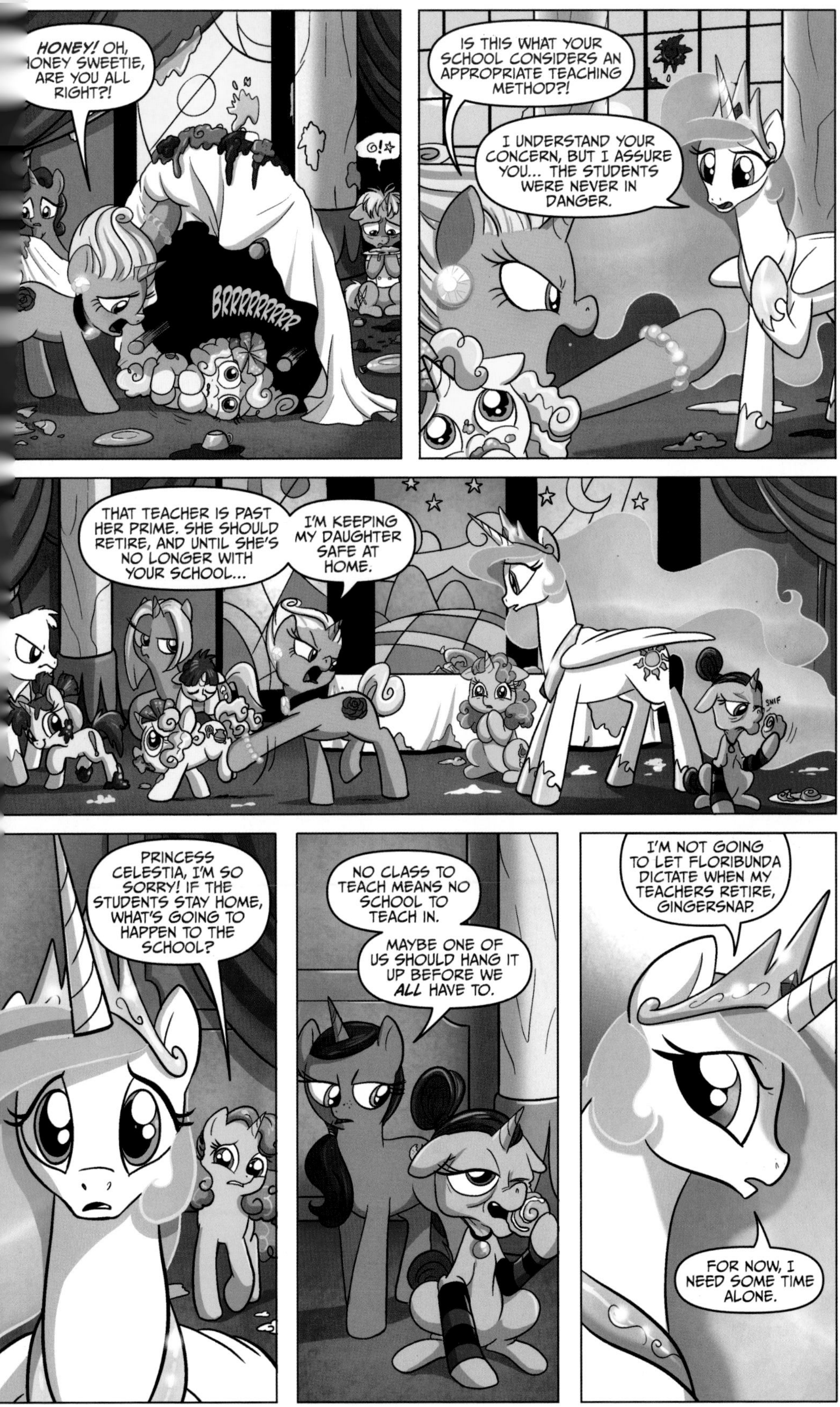
HONEY! OH, HONEY SWEETIE, ARE YOU ALL RIGHT?!
BRRRRRRRRRR
IS THIS WHAT YOUR SCHOOL CONSIDERS AN APPROPRIATE TEACHING METHOD?!
I UNDERSTAND YOUR CONCERN, BUT I ASSURE YOU... THE STUDENTS WERE NEVER IN DANGER.
THAT TEACHER IS PAST HER PRIME. SHE SHOULD RETIRE, AND UNTIL SHE'S NO LONGER WITH YOUR SCHOOL...
I'M KEEPING MY DAUGHTER SAFE AT HOME.
SNIF
PRINCESS CELESTIA, I'M SO SORRY! IF THE STUDENTS STAY HOME, WHAT'S GOING TO HAPPEN TO THE SCHOOL?
NO CLASS TO TEACH MEANS NO SCHOOL TO TEACH IN.
MAYBE ONE OF US SHOULD HANG IT UP BEFORE WE ALL HAVE TO.
I'M NOT GOING TO LET FLORIBUNDA DICTATE WHEN MY TEACHERS RETIRE, GINGERSNAP.
FOR NOW, I NEED SOME TIME ALONE.

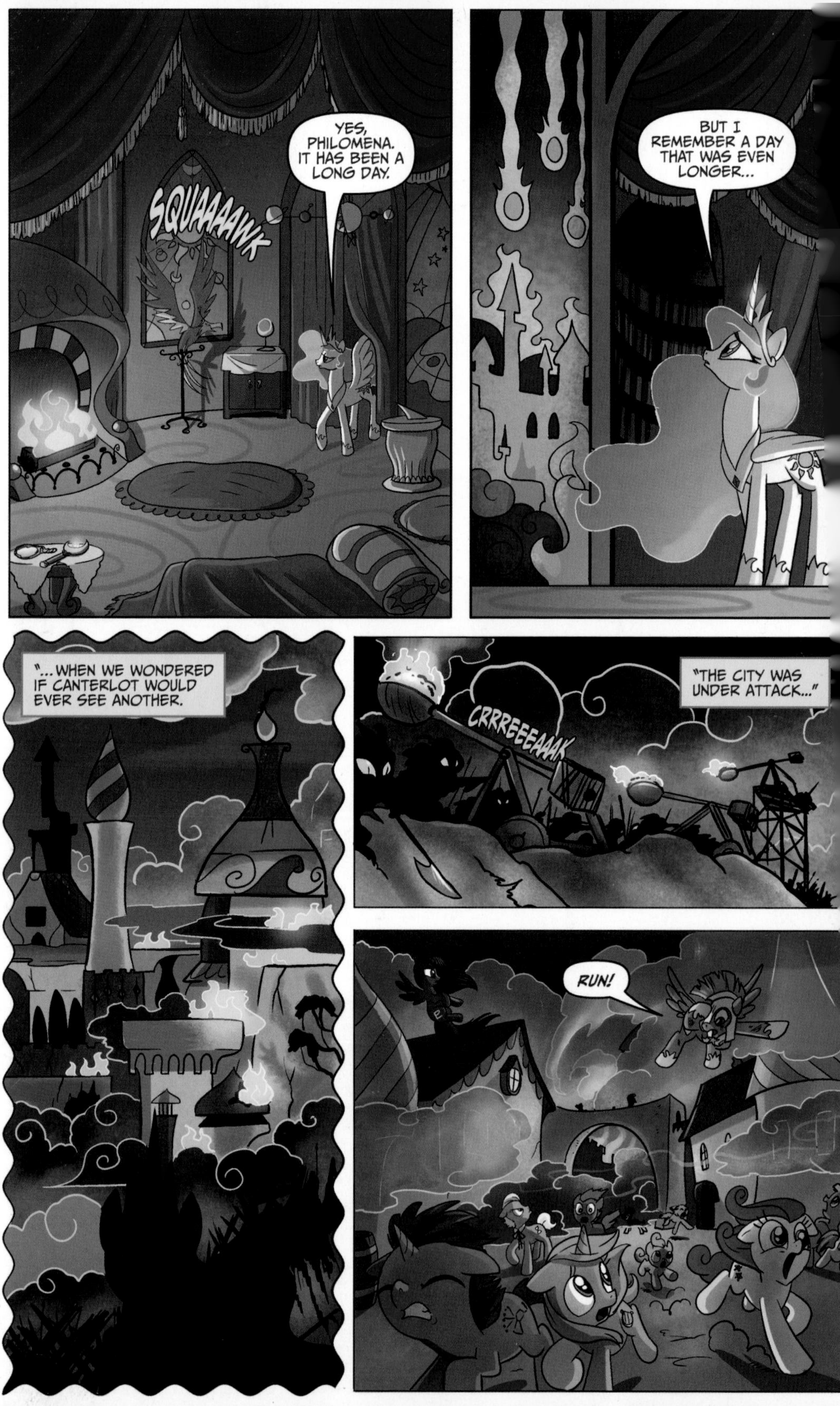
SQUAAAAWK
YES, PHILOMENA. IT HAS BEEN A LONG DAY.
BUT I REMEMBER A DAY THAT WAS EVEN LONGER...
"...WHEN WE WONDERED IF CANTERLOT WOULD EVER SEE ANOTHER.
"THE CITY WAS UNDER ATTACK..."
CRRREEEAAAK
RUN!

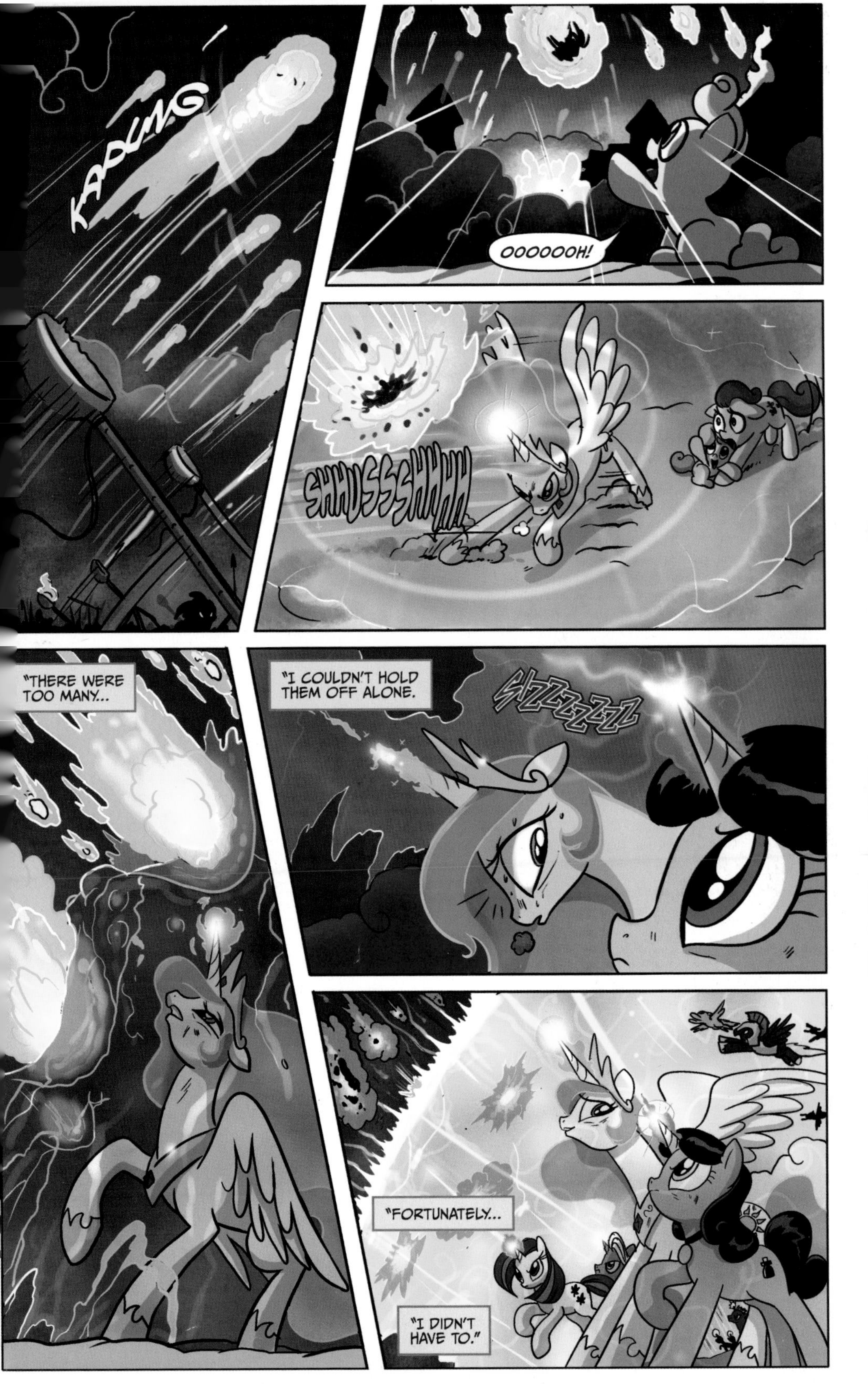
KADUNG
OOOOOOH!
SHHUSSSHHHH
"THERE WERE TOO MANY...
"I COULDN'T HOLD THEM OFF ALONE.
SIZZZZZZZ
"FORTUNATELY...
"I DIDN'T HAVE TO."

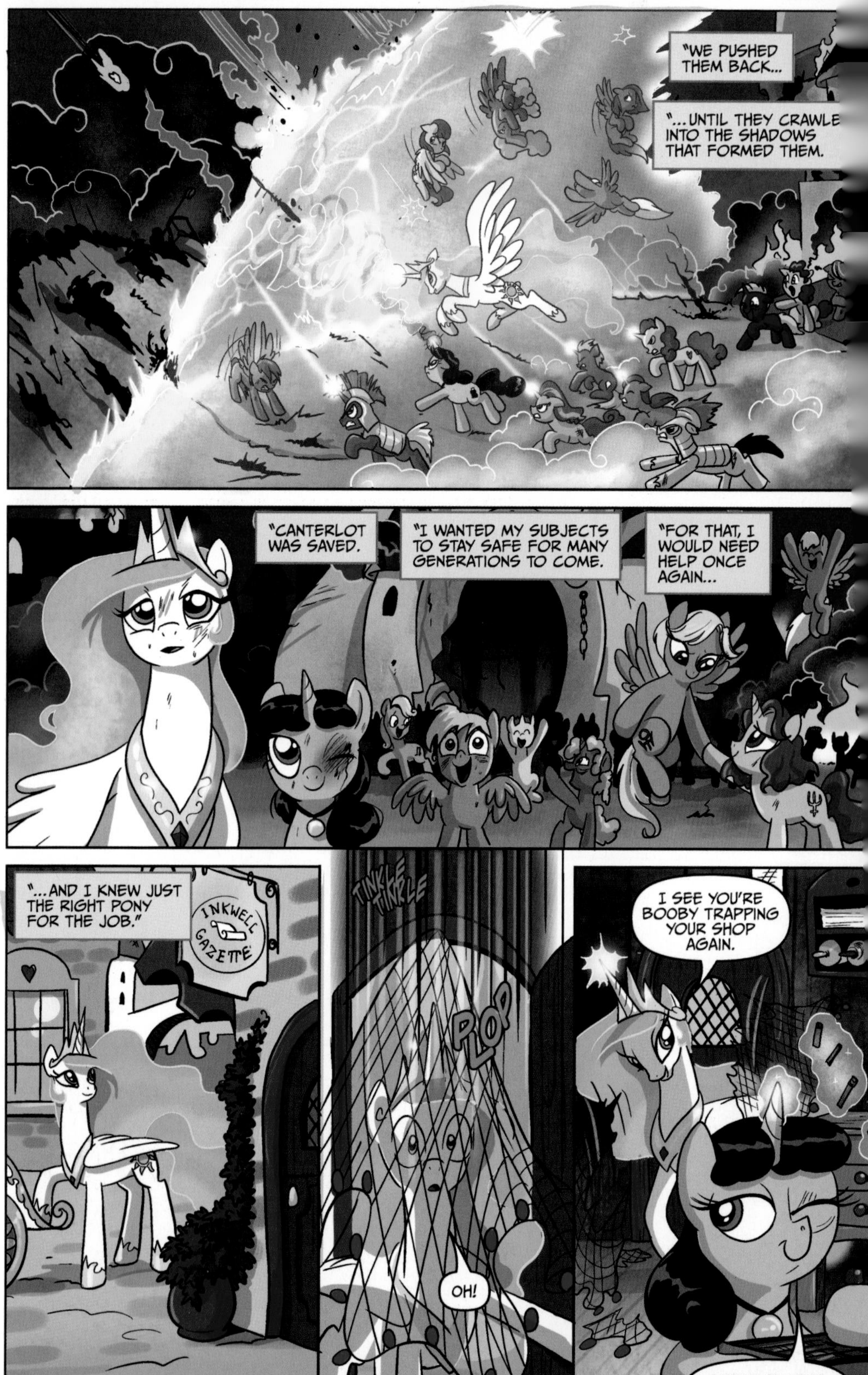
"WE PUSHED THEM BACK...
"...UNTIL THEY CRAWLE INTO THE SHADOWS THAT FORMED THEM.
"CANTERLOT WAS SAVED.
"I WANTED MY SUBJECTS TO STAY SAFE FOR MANY GENERATIONS TO COME.
"FOR THAT, I WOULD NEED HELP ONCE AGAIN...
"...AND I KNEW JUST THE RIGHT PONY FOR THE JOB."
INKWELL GAZETTE
TINKLE TINKLE
PLOP
OH!
I SEE YOU'RE BOOBY TRAPPING YOUR SHOP AGAIN.
LIKE I ALWAYS SAY, "REWARDS GO TO THE WARY."

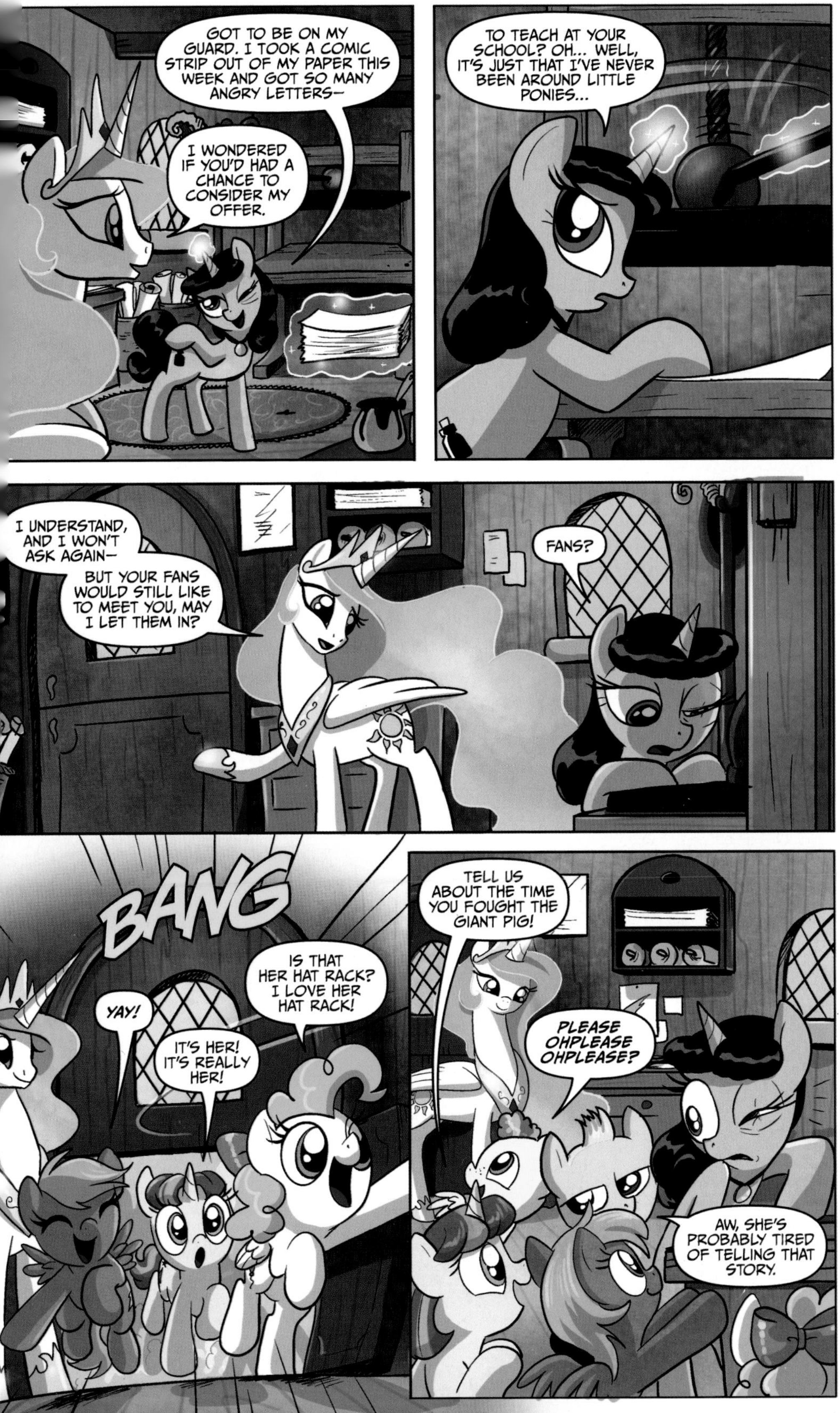

GOT TO BE ON MY GUARD. I TOOK A COMIC STRIP OUT OF MY PAPER THIS WEEK AND GOT SO MANY ANGRY LETTERS—
I WONDERED IF YOU'D HAD A CHANCE TO CONSIDER MY OFFER.
TO TEACH AT YOUR SCHOOL? OH... WELL, IT'S JUST THAT I'VE NEVER BEEN AROUND LITTLE PONIES...
I UNDERSTAND, AND I WON'T ASK AGAIN—
BUT YOUR FANS WOULD STILL LIKE TO MEET YOU, MAY I LET THEM IN?
FANS?
BANG
YAY!
IS THAT HER HAT RACK? I LOVE HER HAT RACK!
IT'S HER! IT'S REALLY HER!
TELL US ABOUT THE TIME YOU FOUGHT THE GIANT PIG!
PLEASE OHPLEASE OHPLEASE?
AW, SHE'S PROBABLY TIRED OF TELLING THAT STORY.

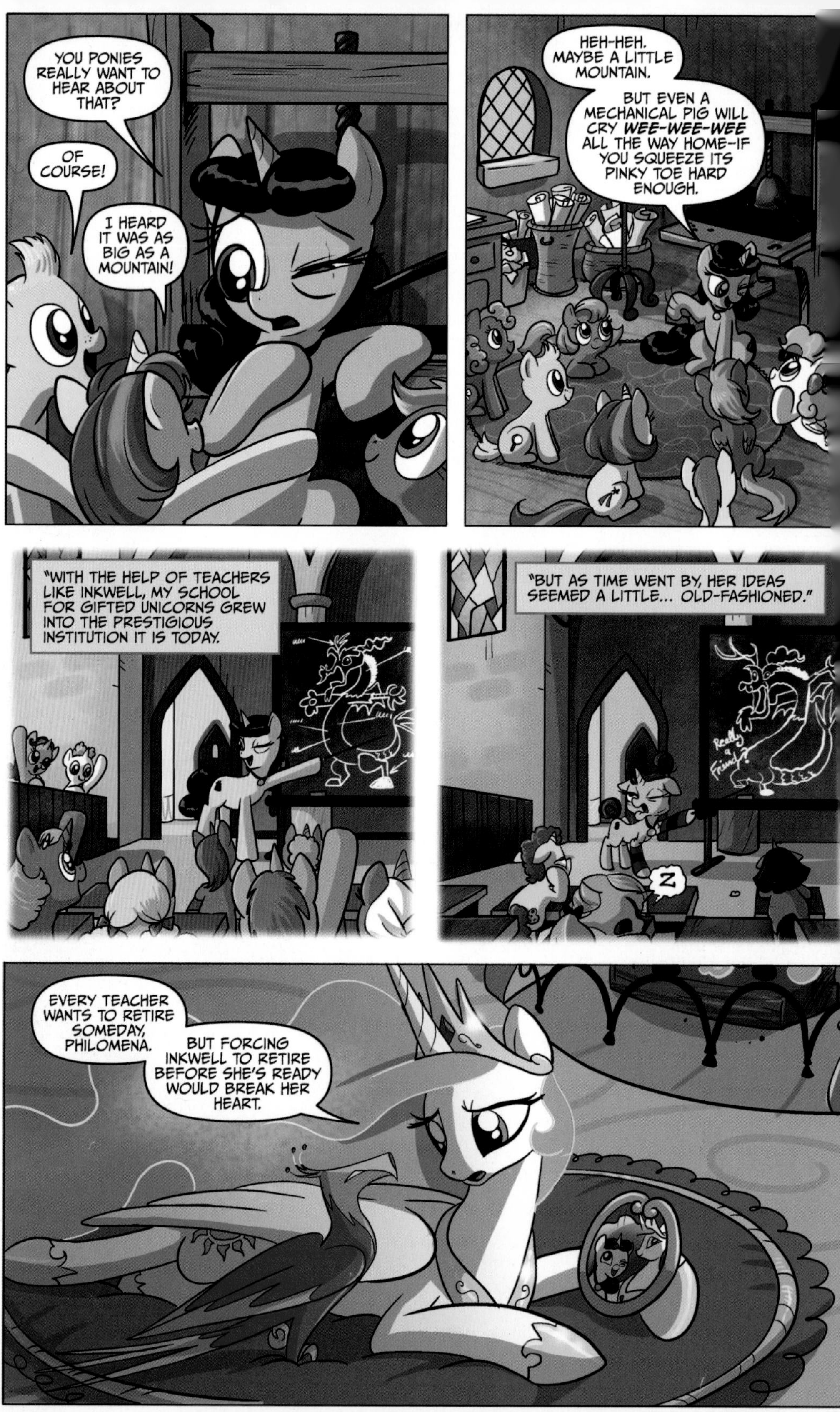
YOU PONIES REALLY WANT TO HEAR ABOUT THAT?
OF COURSE!
I HEARD IT WAS AS BIG AS A MOUNTAIN!
HEH-HEH. MAYBE A LITTLE MOUNTAIN.
BUT EVEN A MECHANICAL PIG WILL CRY **WEE-WEE-WEE** ALL THE WAY HOME—IF YOU SQUEEZE ITS PINKY TOE HARD ENOUGH.
"WITH THE HELP OF TEACHERS LIKE INKWELL, MY SCHOOL FOR GIFTED UNICORNS GREW INTO THE PRESTIGIOUS INSTITUTION IT IS TODAY.
"BUT AS TIME WENT BY, HER IDEAS SEEMED A LITTLE... OLD-FASHIONED."
Really a Friend?
Z
EVERY TEACHER WANTS TO RETIRE SOMEDAY, PHILOMENA.
BUT FORCING INKWELL TO RETIRE BEFORE SHE'S READY WOULD BREAK HER HEART.

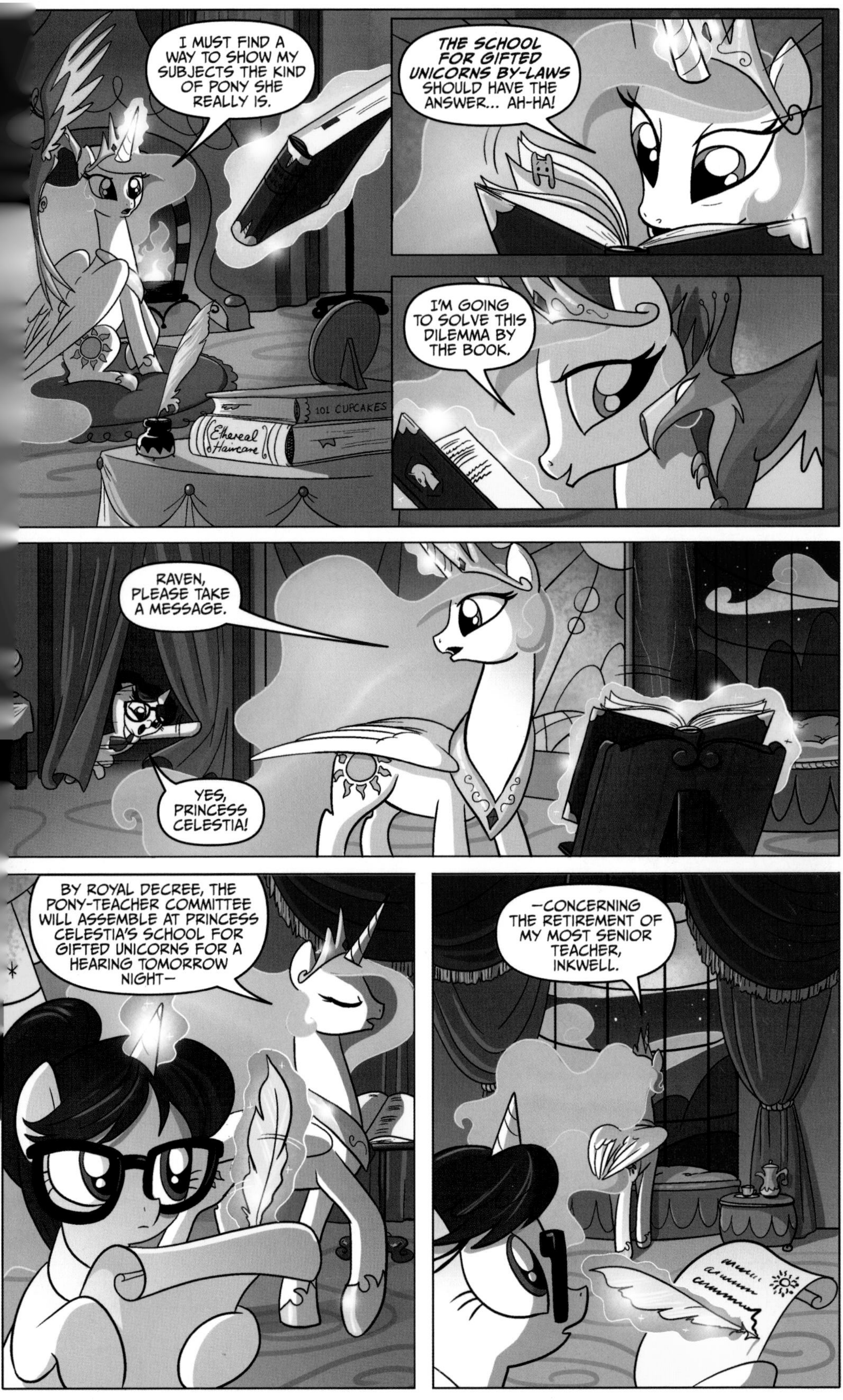
I MUST FIND A WAY TO SHOW MY SUBJECTS THE KIND OF PONY SHE REALLY IS.
101 CUPCAKES
Ethereal Haircare
THE SCHOOL FOR GIFTED UNICORNS BY-LAWS SHOULD HAVE THE ANSWER... AH-HA!
I'M GOING TO SOLVE THIS DILEMMA BY THE BOOK.
RAVEN, PLEASE TAKE A MESSAGE.
YES, PRINCESS CELESTIA!
BY ROYAL DECREE, THE PONY-TEACHER COMMITTEE WILL ASSEMBLE AT PRINCESS CELESTIA'S SCHOOL FOR GIFTED UNICORNS FOR A HEARING TOMORROW NIGHT–
–CONCERNING THE RETIREMENT OF MY MOST SENIOR TEACHER, INKWELL.

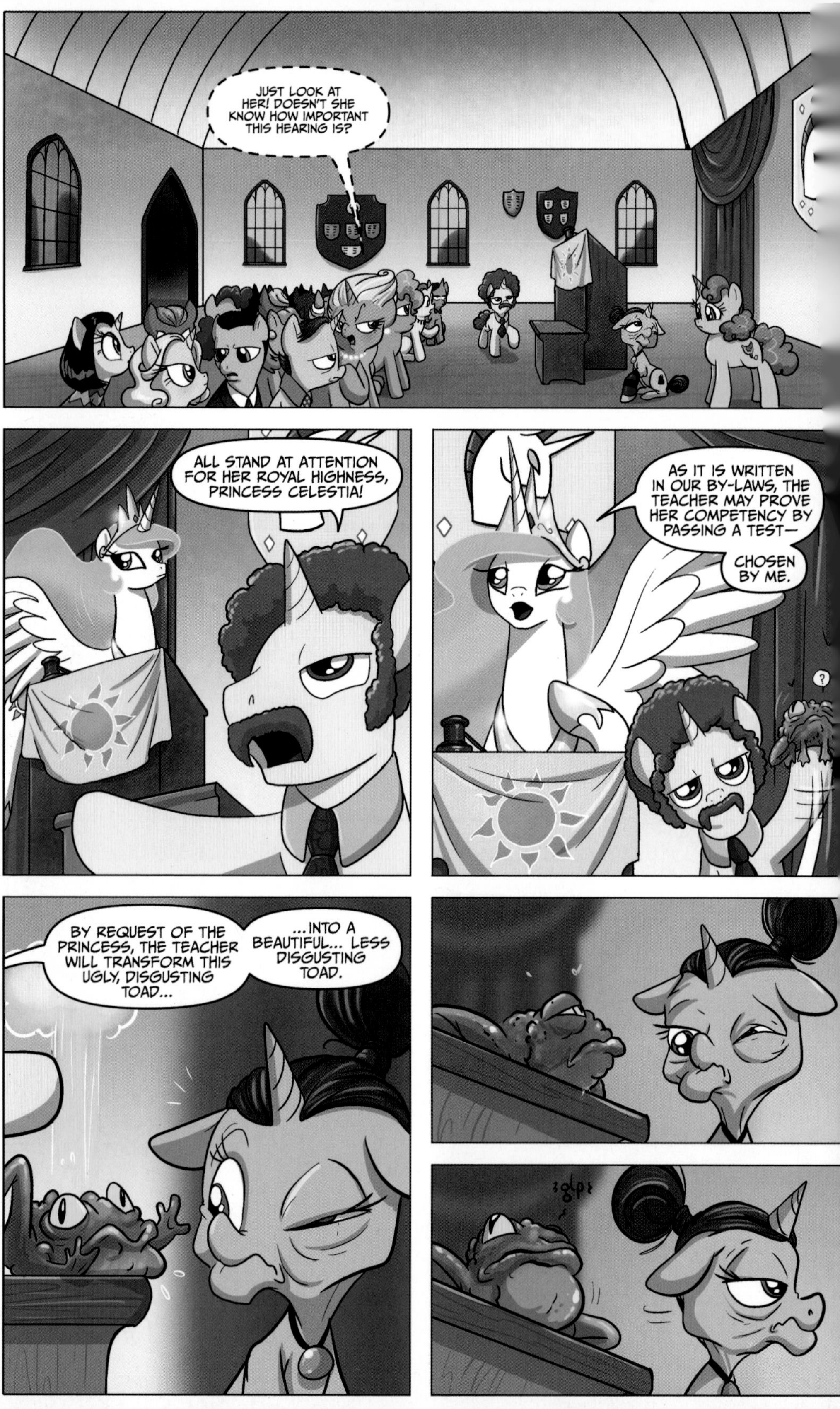
JUST LOOK AT HER! DOESN'T SHE KNOW HOW IMPORTANT THIS HEARING IS?
ALL STAND AT ATTENTION FOR HER ROYAL HIGHNESS, PRINCESS CELESTIA!
AS IT IS WRITTEN IN OUR BY-LAWS, THE TEACHER MAY PROVE HER COMPETENCY BY PASSING A TEST—
CHOSEN BY ME.
?
BY REQUEST OF THE PRINCESS, THE TEACHER WILL TRANSFORM THIS UGLY, DISGUSTING TOAD...
...INTO A BEAUTIFUL... LESS DISGUSTING TOAD.
glp

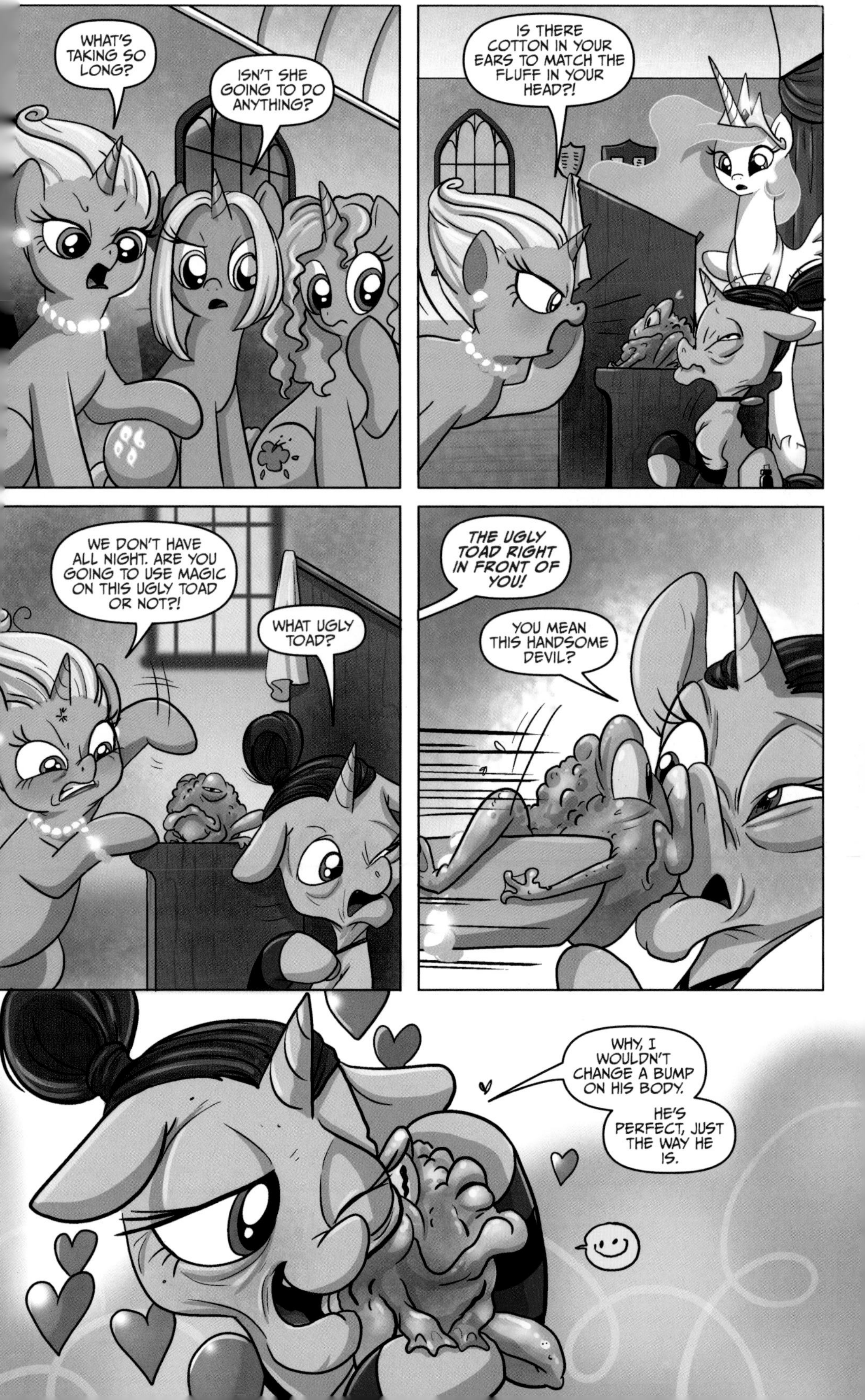
WHAT'S TAKING SO LONG?
ISN'T SHE GOING TO DO ANYTHING?
IS THERE COTTON IN YOUR EARS TO MATCH THE FLUFF IN YOUR HEAD?!
WE DON'T HAVE ALL NIGHT. ARE YOU GOING TO USE MAGIC ON THIS UGLY TOAD OR NOT?!
WHAT UGLY TOAD?
THE UGLY TOAD RIGHT IN FRONT OF YOU!
YOU MEAN THIS HANDSOME DEVIL?
WHY, I WOULDN'T CHANGE A BUMP ON HIS BODY.
HE'S PERFECT, JUST THE WAY HE IS.

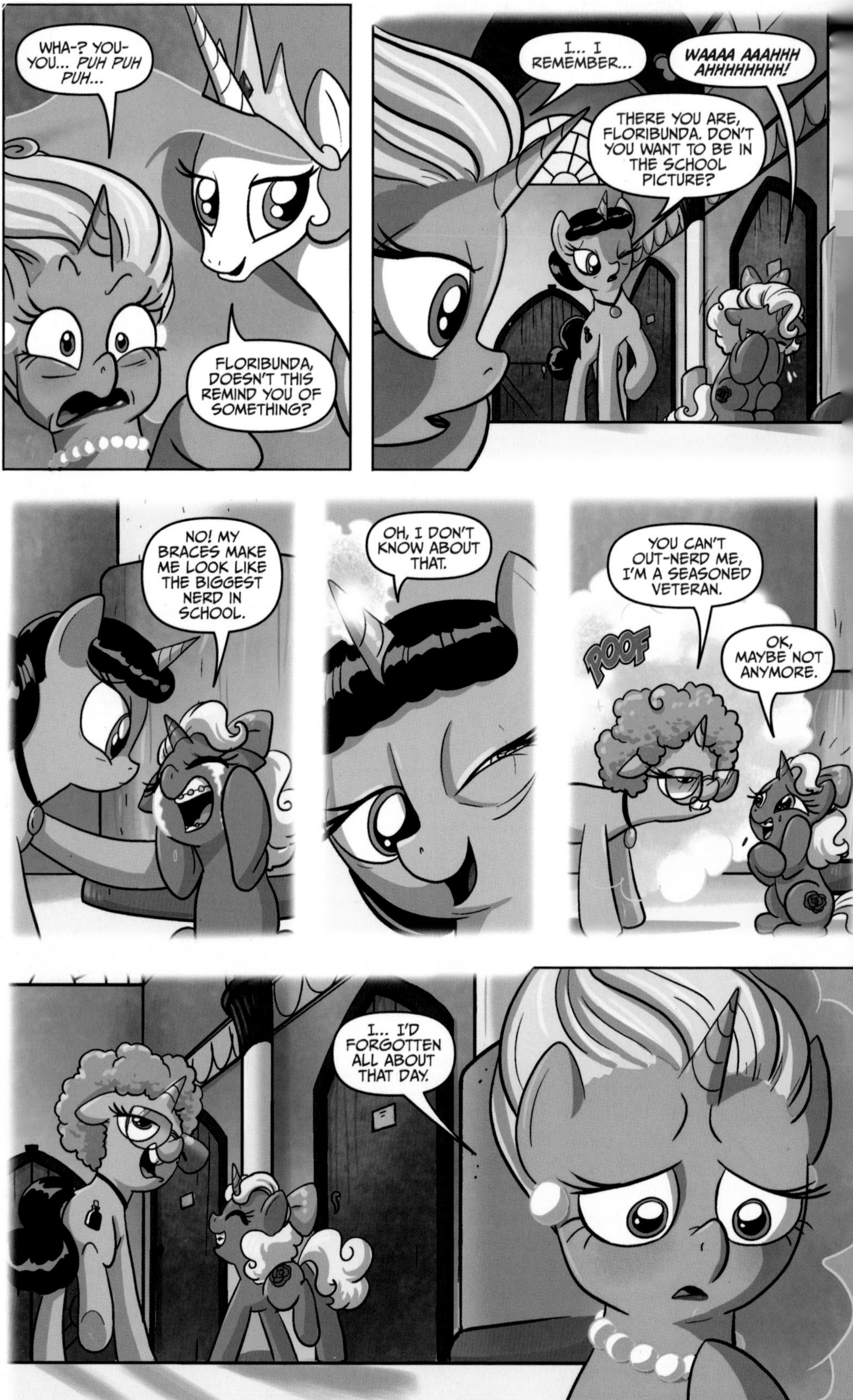
WHA-? YOU- YOU... PUH PUH PUH...
FLORIBUNDA, DOESN'T THIS REMIND YOU OF SOMETHING?
I... I REMEMBER...
WAAAA AAAHHH AHHHHHHHH!
THERE YOU ARE, FLORIBUNDA. DON'T YOU WANT TO BE IN THE SCHOOL PICTURE?
NO! MY BRACES MAKE ME LOOK LIKE THE BIGGEST NERD IN SCHOOL.
OH, I DON'T KNOW ABOUT THAT.
POOF
YOU CAN'T OUT-NERD ME, I'M A SEASONED VETERAN.
OK, MAYBE NOT ANYMORE.
I... I'D FORGOTTEN ALL ABOUT THAT DAY.

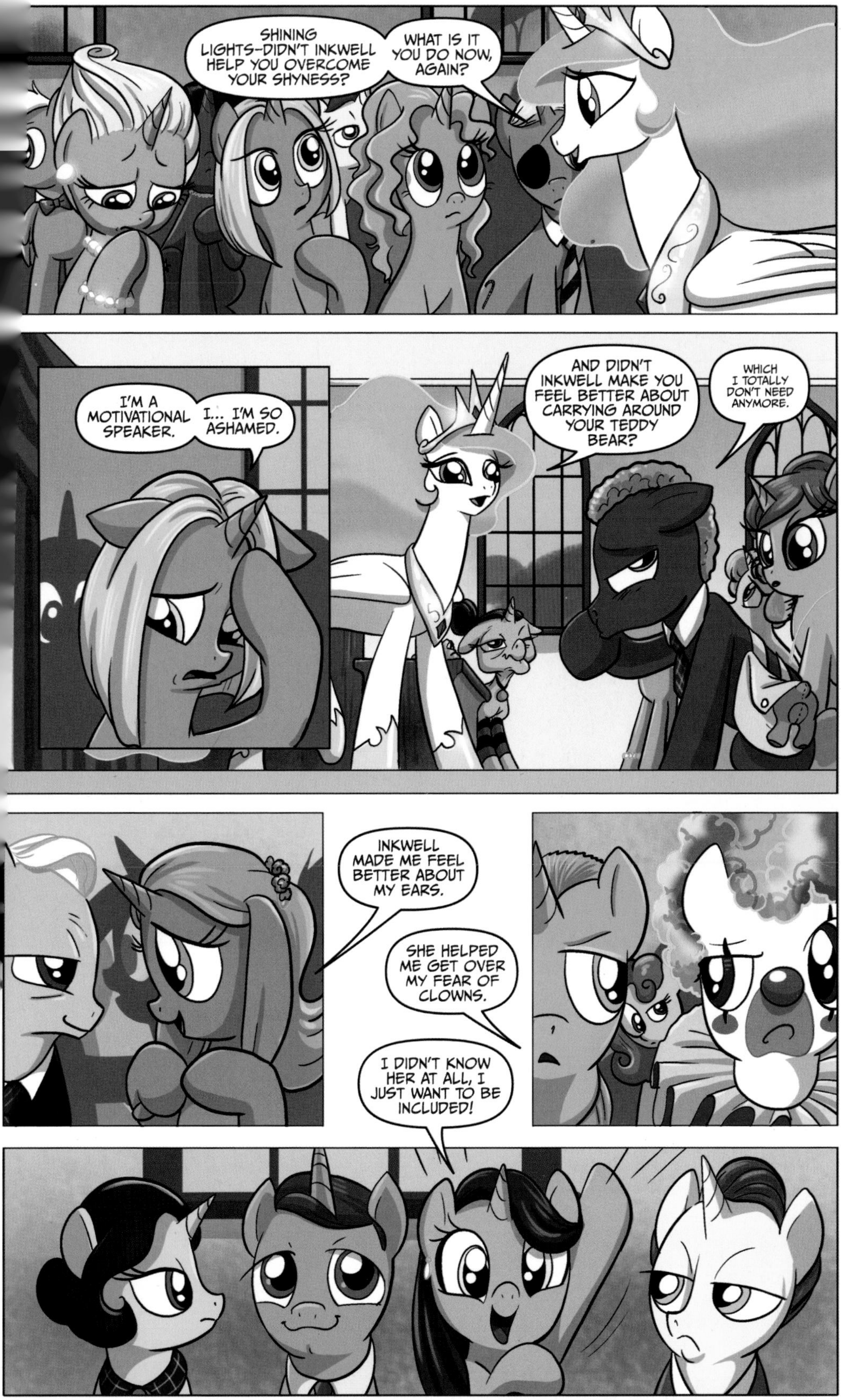
SHINING LIGHTS–DIDN'T INKWELL HELP YOU OVERCOME YOUR SHYNESS?
WHAT IS IT YOU DO NOW, AGAIN?
I'M A MOTIVATIONAL SPEAKER.
I... I'M SO ASHAMED.
AND DIDN'T INKWELL MAKE YOU FEEL BETTER ABOUT CARRYING AROUND YOUR TEDDY BEAR?
WHICH I TOTALLY DON'T NEED ANYMORE.
INKWELL MADE ME FEEL BETTER ABOUT MY EARS.
SHE HELPED ME GET OVER MY FEAR OF CLOWNS.
I DIDN'T KNOW HER AT ALL, I JUST WANT TO BE INCLUDED!

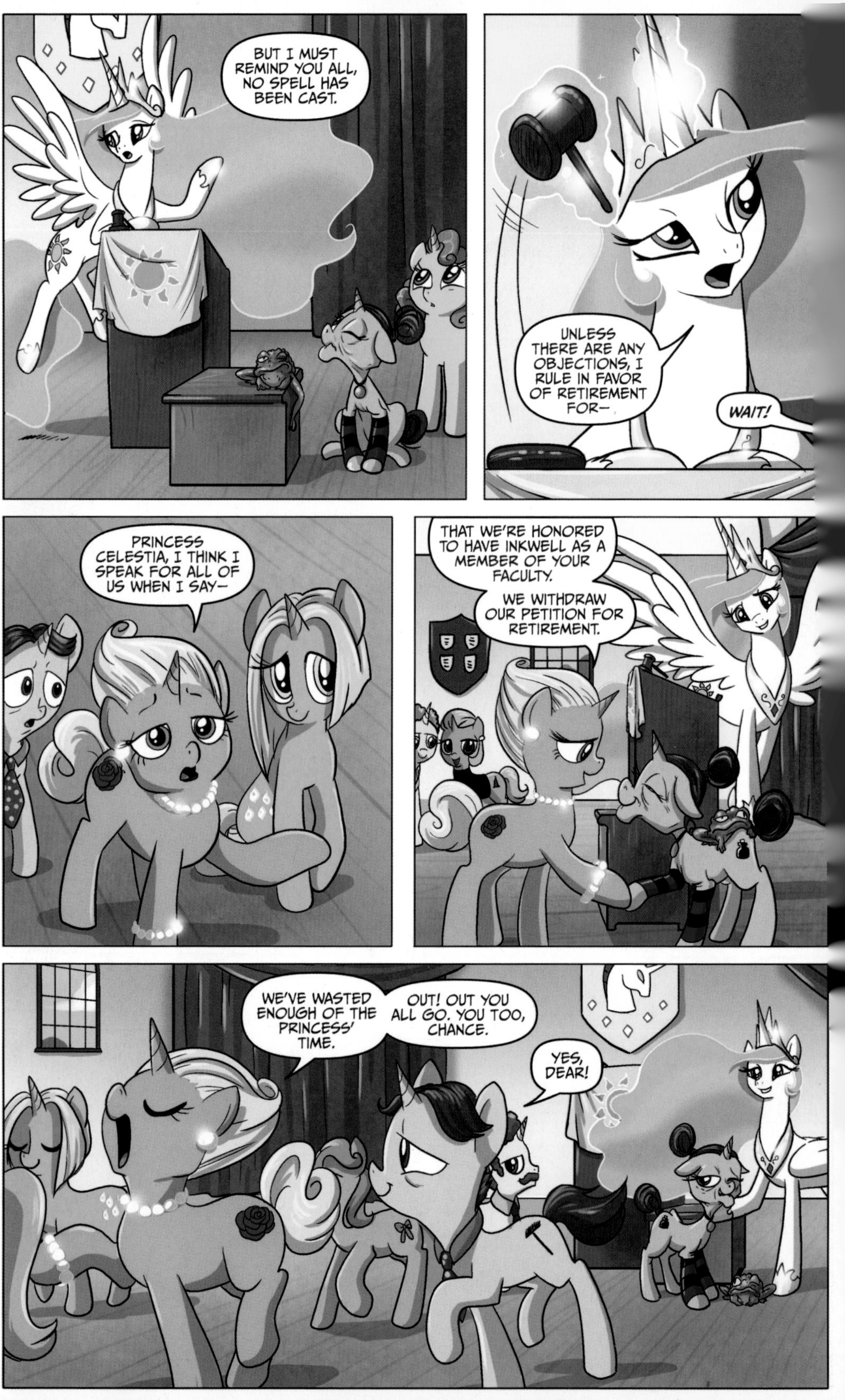
BUT I MUST REMIND YOU ALL, NO SPELL HAS BEEN CAST.
UNLESS THERE ARE ANY OBJECTIONS, I RULE IN FAVOR OF RETIREMENT FOR—
WAIT!
PRINCESS CELESTIA, I THINK I SPEAK FOR ALL OF US WHEN I SAY—
THAT WE'RE HONORED TO HAVE INKWELL AS A MEMBER OF YOUR FACULTY.
WE WITHDRAW OUR PETITION FOR RETIREMENT.
WE'VE WASTED ENOUGH OF THE PRINCESS' TIME.
OUT! OUT YOU ALL GO. YOU TOO, CHANCE.
YES, DEAR!

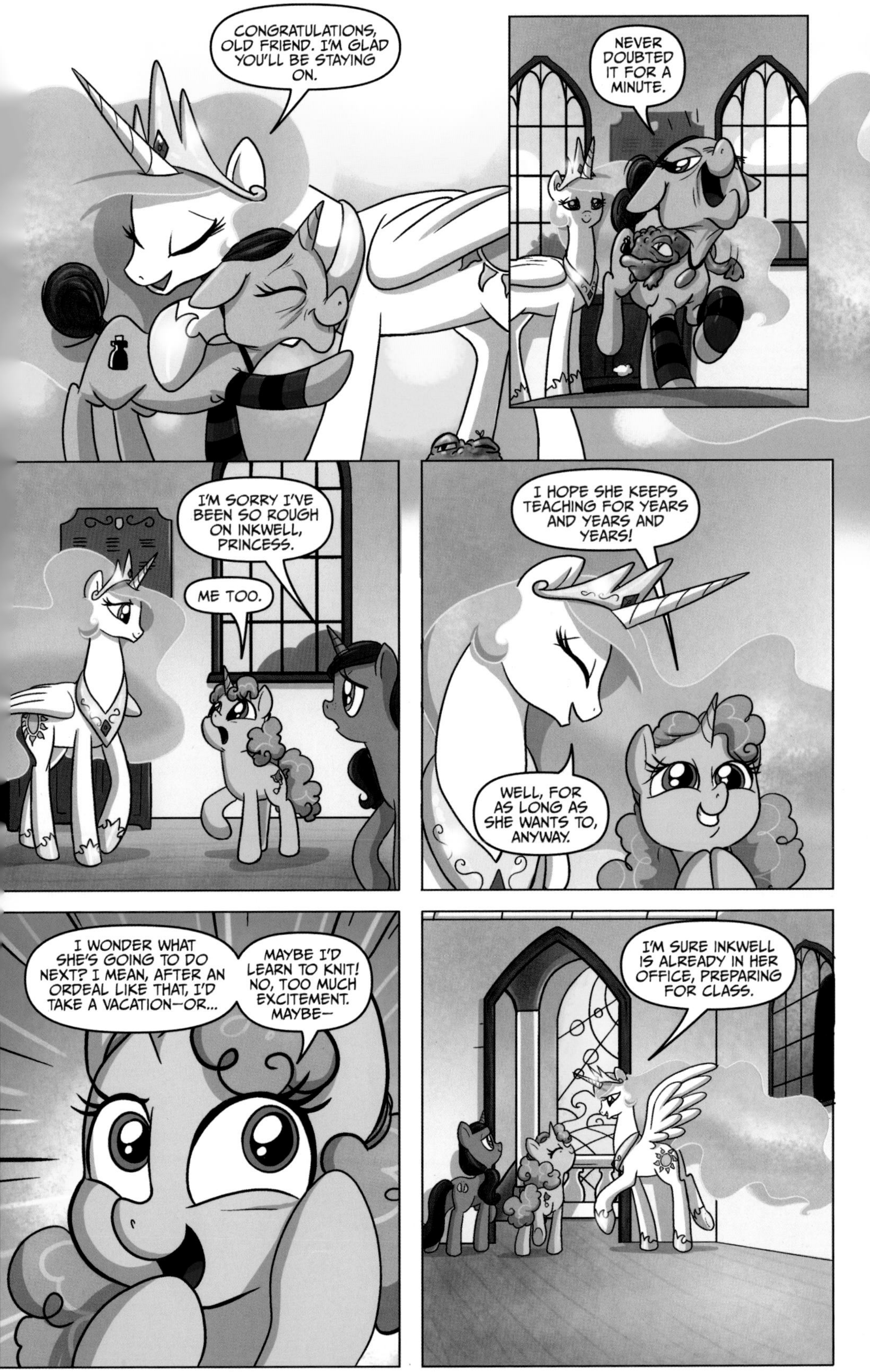
CONGRATULATIONS, OLD FRIEND. I'M GLAD YOU'LL BE STAYING ON.
NEVER DOUBTED IT FOR A MINUTE.
I'M SORRY I'VE BEEN SO ROUGH ON INKWELL, PRINCESS.
ME TOO.
I HOPE SHE KEEPS TEACHING FOR YEARS AND YEARS AND YEARS!
WELL, FOR AS LONG AS SHE WANTS TO, ANYWAY.
I WONDER WHAT SHE'S GOING TO DO NEXT? I MEAN, AFTER AN ORDEAL LIKE THAT, I'D TAKE A VACATION—OR...
MAYBE I'D LEARN TO KNIT! NO, TOO MUCH EXCITEMENT. MAYBE—
I'M SURE INKWELL IS ALREADY IN HER OFFICE, PREPARING FOR CLASS.

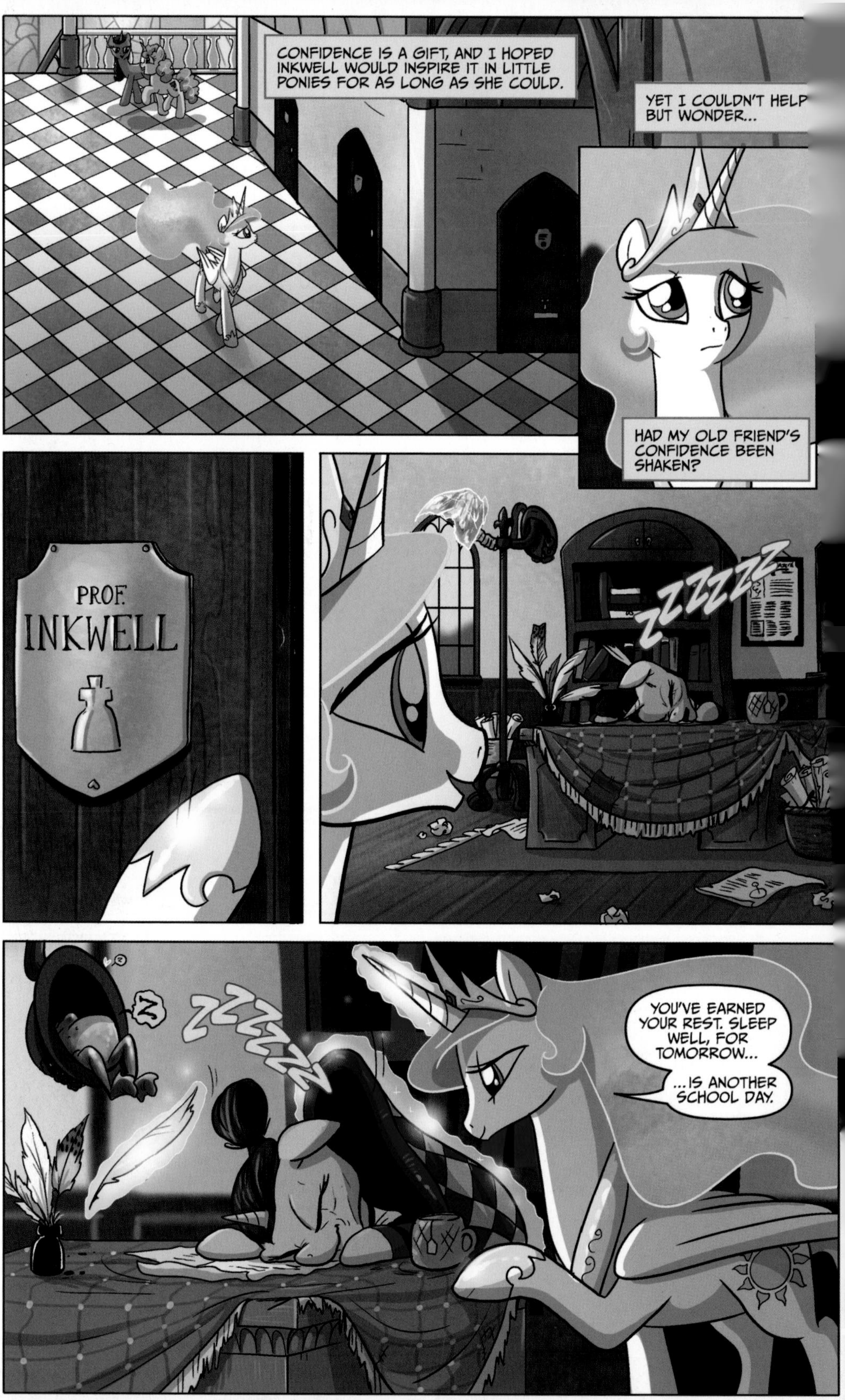
CONFIDENCE IS A GIFT, AND I HOPED INKWELL WOULD INSPIRE IT IN LITTLE PONIES FOR AS LONG AS SHE COULD.
YET I COULDN'T HELP BUT WONDER...
HAD MY OLD FRIEND'S CONFIDENCE BEEN SHAKEN?
PROF. INKWELL
ZZZZZZ
ZZZZZZ
Z
YOU'VE EARNED YOUR REST. SLEEP WELL, FOR TOMORROW...
...IS ANOTHER SCHOOL DAY.

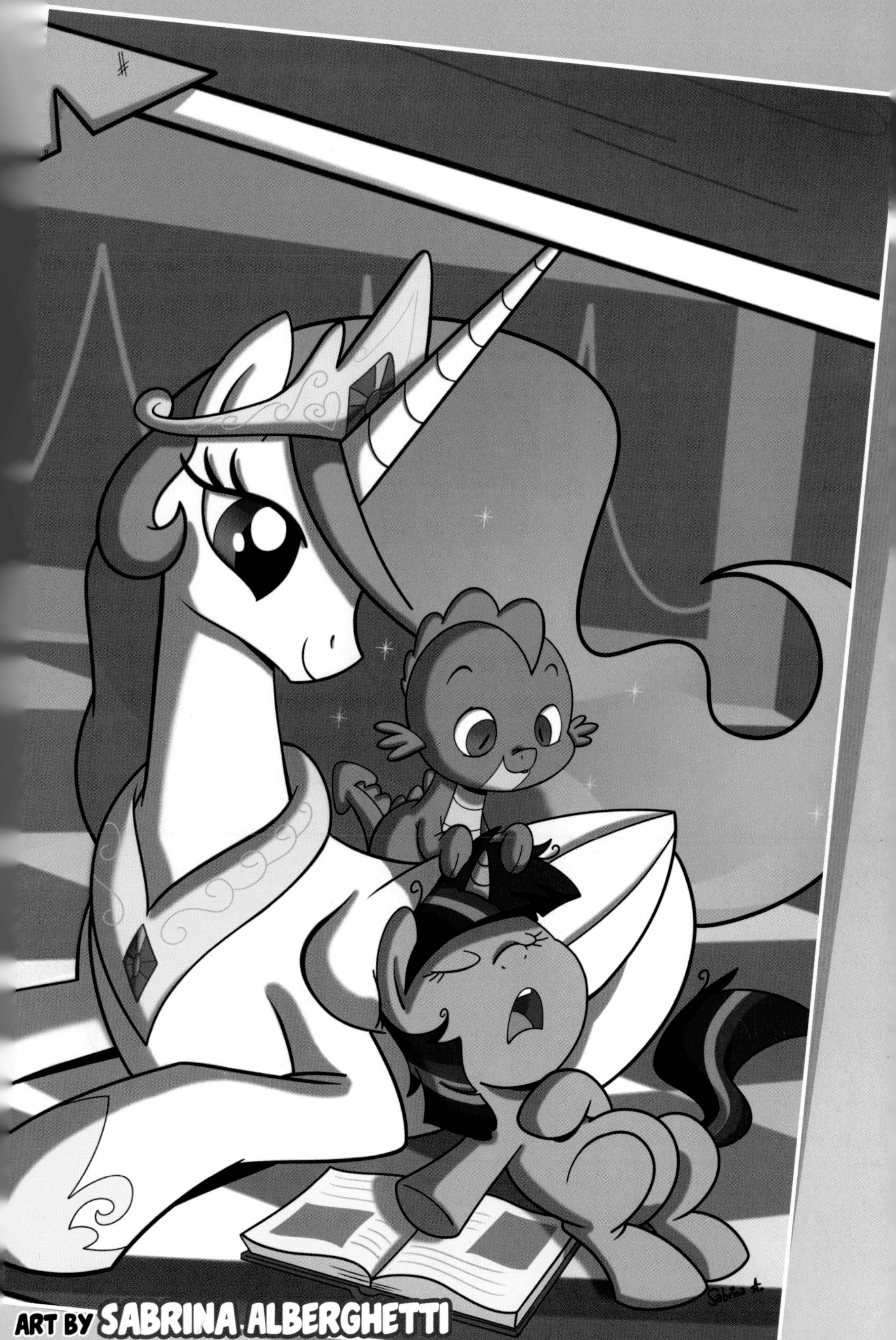
Sabrina A.

ART BY SABRINA ALBERGHETTI

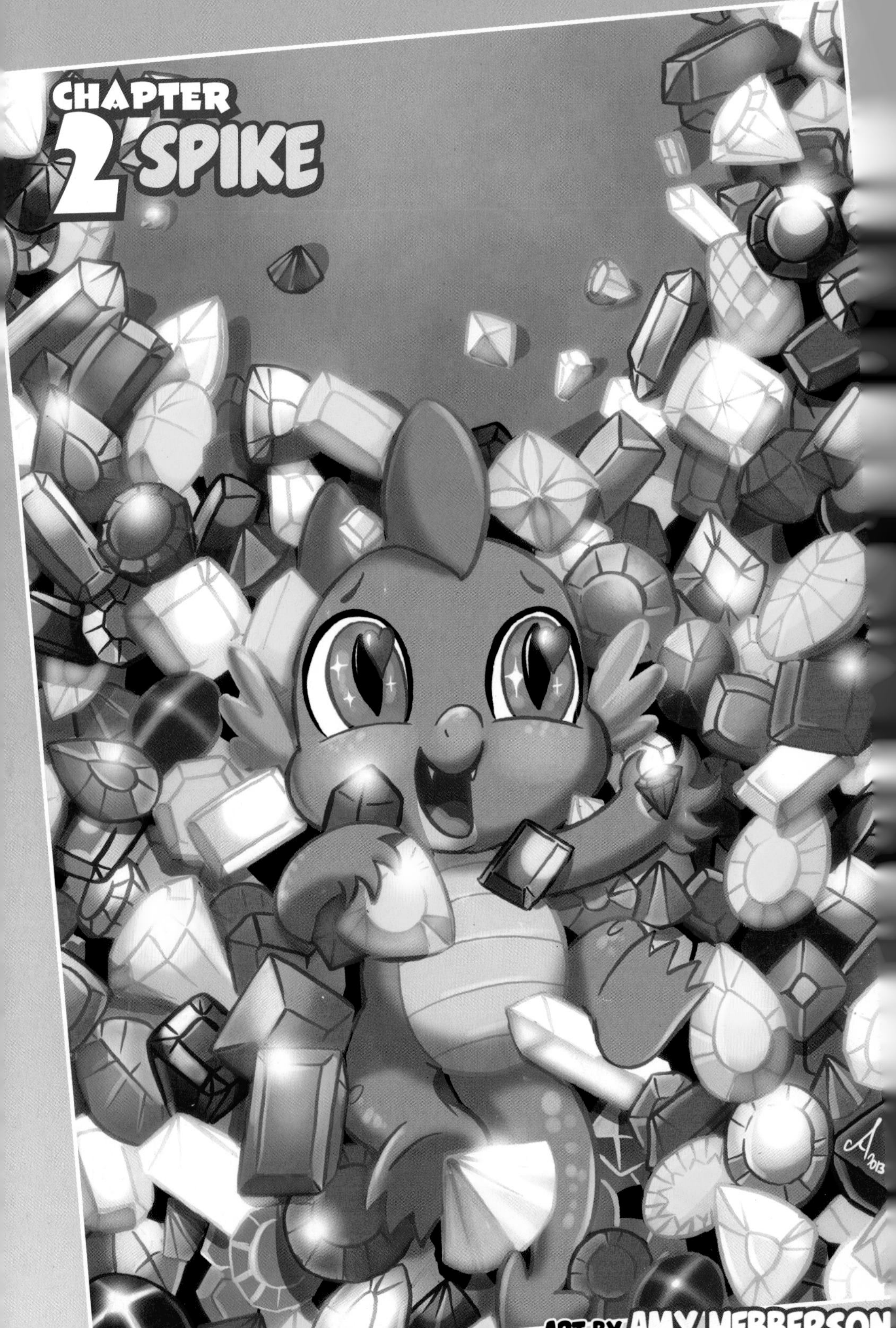
CHAPTER
2 SPIKE
ART BY AMY MEBBERSON

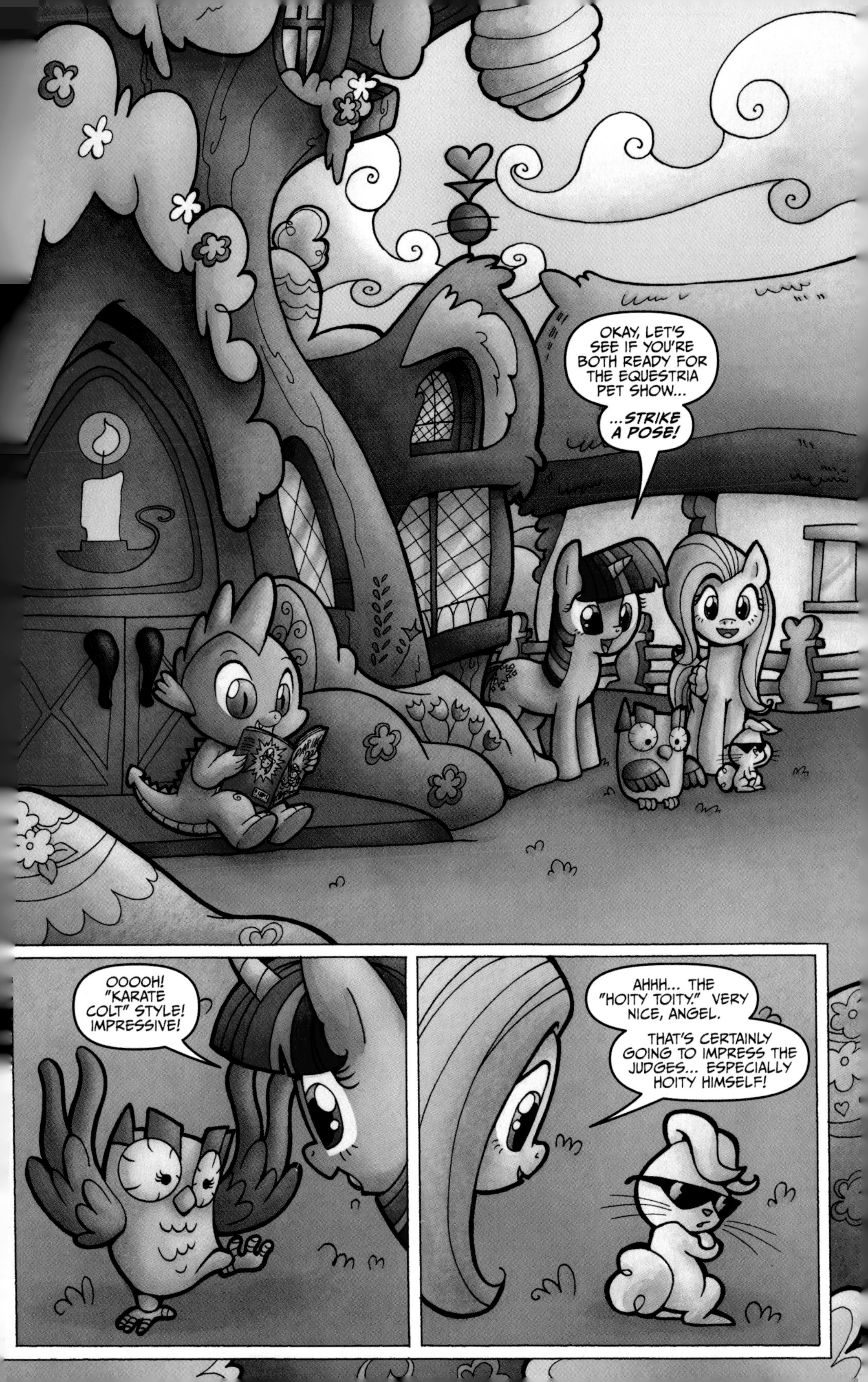
OKAY, LET'S SEE IF YOU'RE BOTH READY FOR THE EQUESTRIA PET SHOW...
...STRIKE A POSE!
OOOOH! "KARATE COLT" STYLE! IMPRESSIVE!
AHHH... THE "HOITY TOITY." VERY NICE, ANGEL.
THAT'S CERTAINLY GOING TO IMPRESS THE JUDGES... ESPECIALLY HOITY HIMSELF!

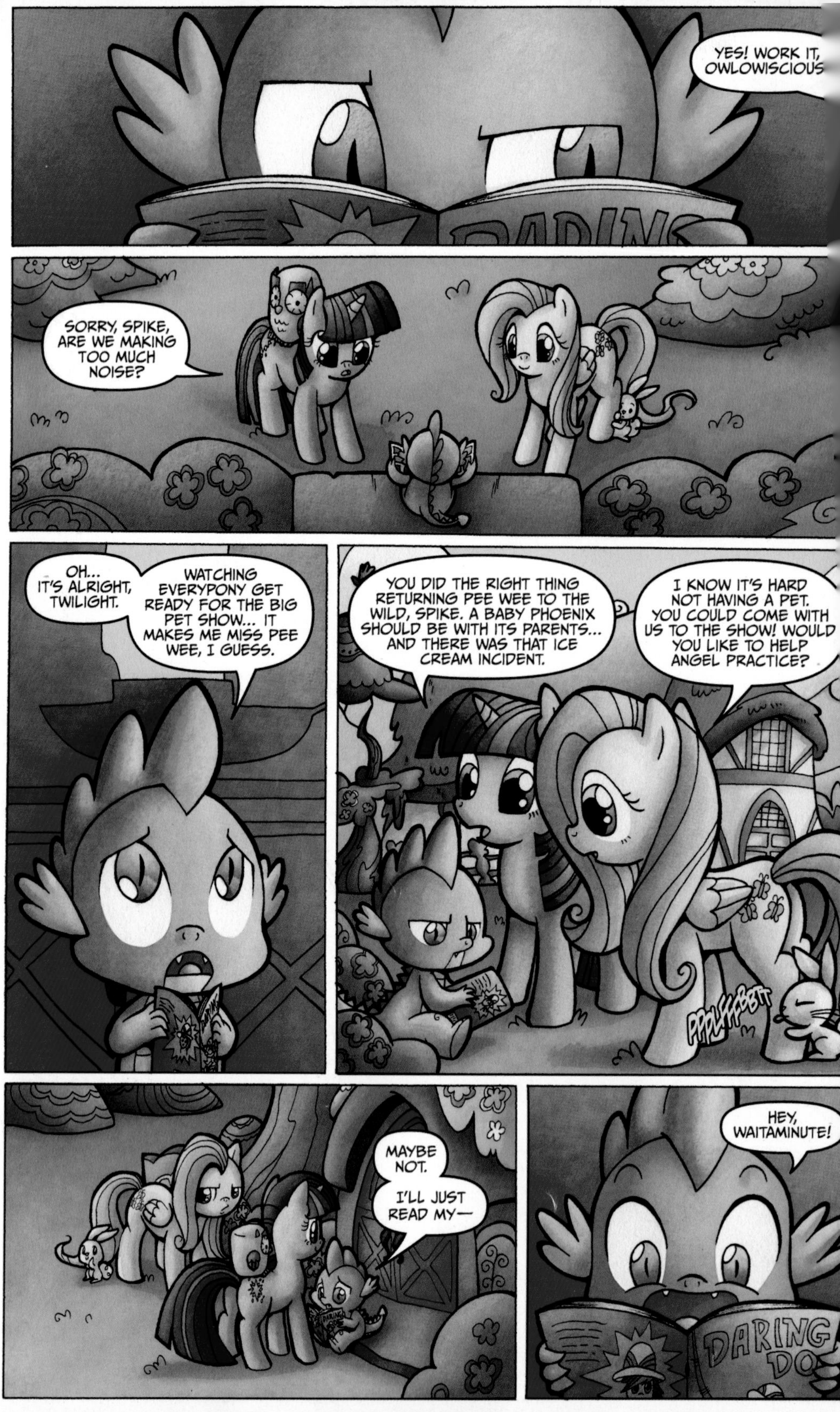
YES! WORK IT, OWLOWISCIOUS
DARING
SORRY, SPIKE, ARE WE MAKING TOO MUCH NOISE?
OH... IT'S ALRIGHT, TWILIGHT.
WATCHING EVERYPONY GET READY FOR THE BIG PET SHOW... IT MAKES ME MISS PEE WEE, I GUESS.
YOU DID THE RIGHT THING RETURNING PEE WEE TO THE WILD, SPIKE. A BABY PHOENIX SHOULD BE WITH ITS PARENTS... AND THERE WAS THAT ICE CREAM INCIDENT.
I KNOW IT'S HARD NOT HAVING A PET. YOU COULD COME WITH US TO THE SHOW! WOULD YOU LIKE TO HELP ANGEL PRACTICE?
PPPLLFFBBTT
MAYBE NOT.
I'LL JUST READ MY—
HEY, WAITAMINUTE!
DARING DO

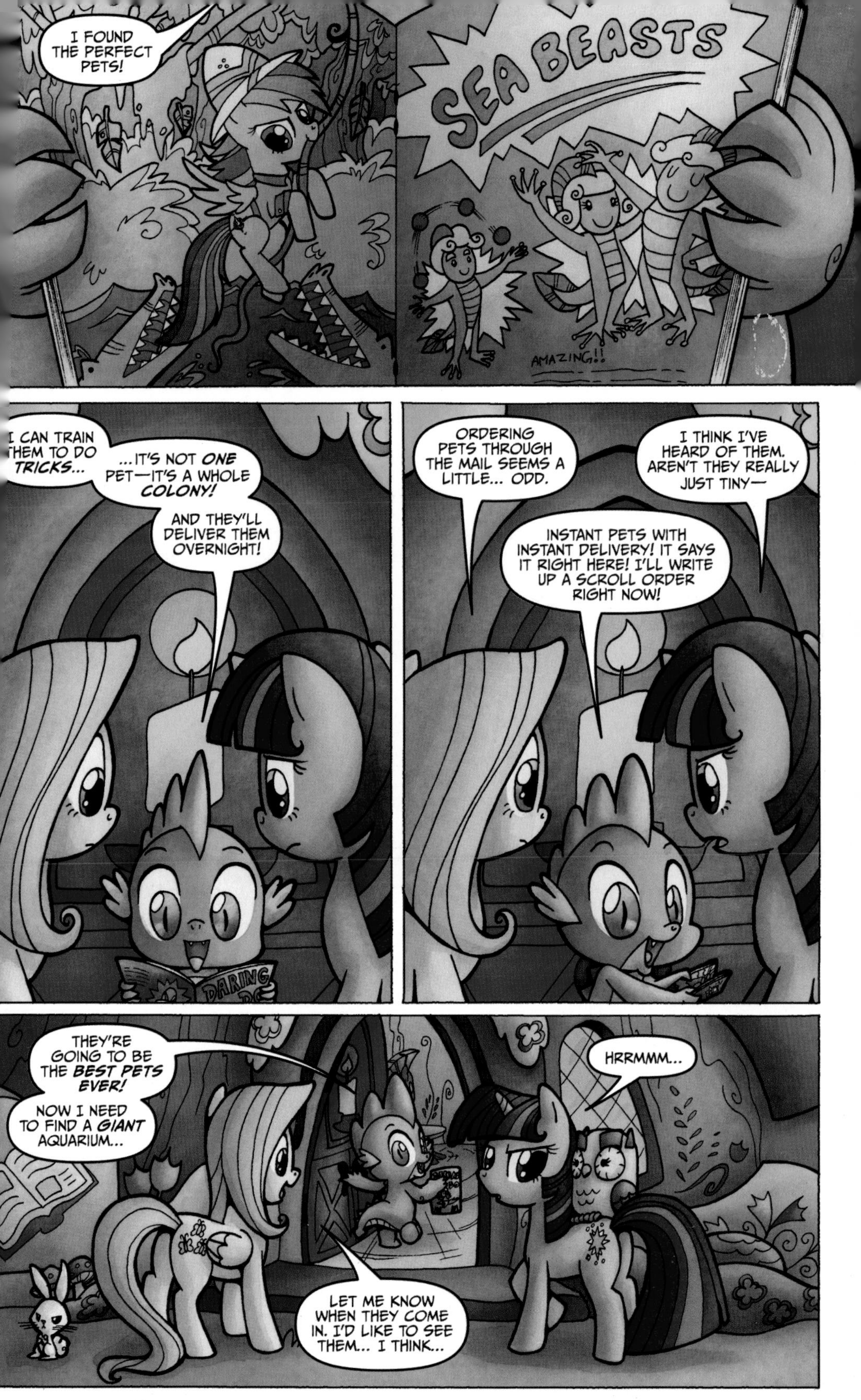
I FOUND THE PERFECT PETS!
SEA BEASTS
AMAZING!!
I CAN TRAIN THEM TO DO TRICKS...
...IT'S NOT ONE PET—IT'S A WHOLE COLONY!
AND THEY'LL DELIVER THEM OVERNIGHT!
DARING DO
ORDERING PETS THROUGH THE MAIL SEEMS A LITTLE... ODD.
I THINK I'VE HEARD OF THEM. AREN'T THEY REALLY JUST TINY—
INSTANT PETS WITH INSTANT DELIVERY! IT SAYS IT RIGHT HERE! I'LL WRITE UP A SCROLL ORDER RIGHT NOW!
THEY'RE GOING TO BE THE BEST PETS EVER!
NOW I NEED TO FIND A GIANT AQUARIUM...
HRRMMM...
LET ME KNOW WHEN THEY COME IN. I'D LIKE TO SEE THEM... I THINK...

THE NEXT DAY...

PONY EXPRESS!

KNOCK KNOCK

THEY'RE HERE!

DELIVERY FOR—

SPIKE! THAT'S ME! THANKS!

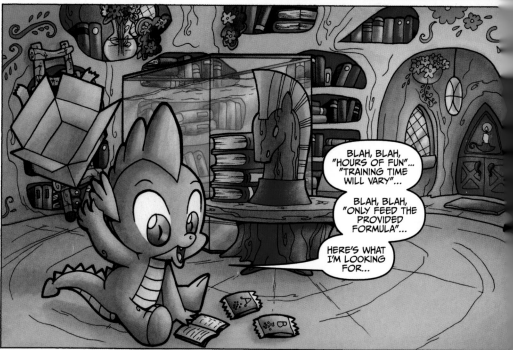

BLAH, BLAH, "HOURS OF FUN"... "TRAINING TIME WILL VARY"...

BLAH, BLAH, "ONLY FEED THE PROVIDED FORMULA"...

HERE'S WHAT I'M LOOKING FOR...

"ADD SEA BEAST EGGS TO WATER... AND LET SIT COVERED FOR THREE HOURS."

WAIT'LL I SHOW THE OTHERS!

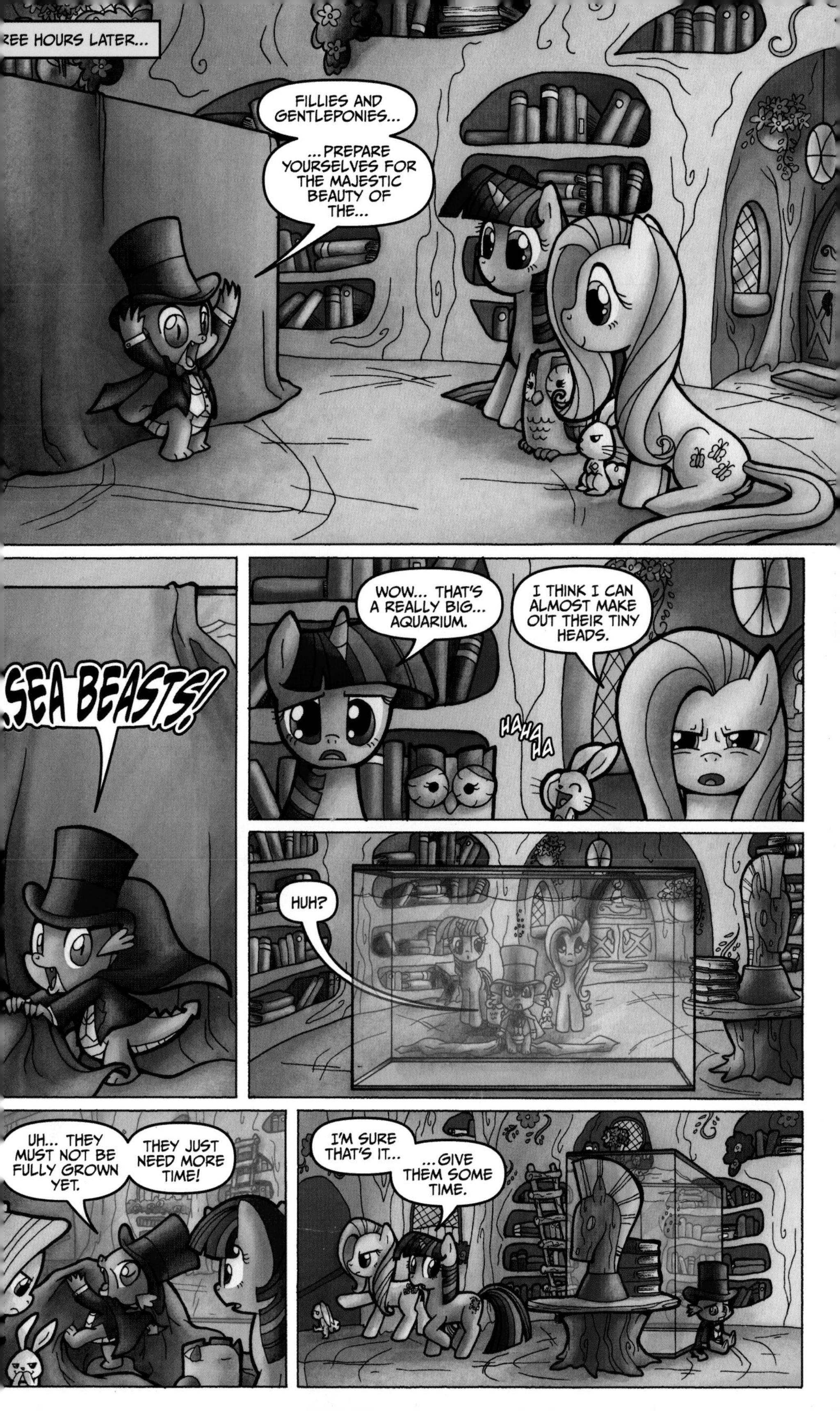

REE HOURS LATER...
FILLIES AND GENTLEPONIES...
...PREPARE YOURSELVES FOR THE MAJESTIC BEAUTY OF THE...
...SEA BEASTS!
WOW... THAT'S A REALLY BIG... AQUARIUM.
I THINK I CAN ALMOST MAKE OUT THEIR TINY HEADS.
HAHAHA
HUH?
UH... THEY MUST NOT BE FULLY GROWN YET.
THEY JUST NEED MORE TIME!
I'M SURE THAT'S IT...
...GIVE THEM SOME TIME.

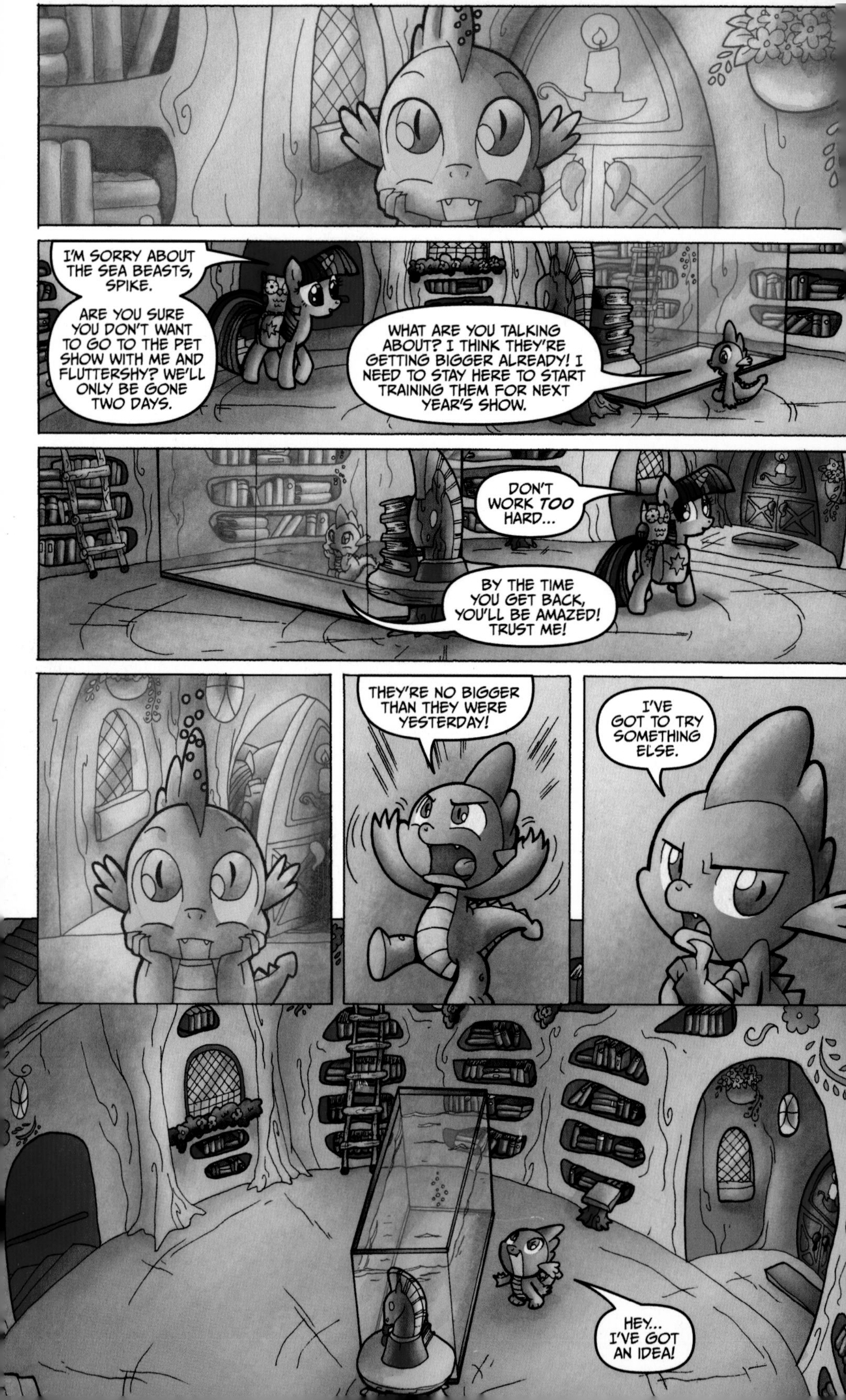
I'M SORRY ABOUT THE SEA BEASTS, SPIKE.
ARE YOU SURE YOU DON'T WANT TO GO TO THE PET SHOW WITH ME AND FLUTTERSHY? WE'LL ONLY BE GONE TWO DAYS.
WHAT ARE YOU TALKING ABOUT? I THINK THEY'RE GETTING BIGGER ALREADY! I NEED TO STAY HERE TO START TRAINING THEM FOR NEXT YEAR'S SHOW.
DON'T WORK *TOO* HARD...
BY THE TIME YOU GET BACK, YOU'LL BE AMAZED! TRUST ME!
THEY'RE NO BIGGER THAN THEY WERE YESTERDAY!
I'VE GOT TO TRY SOMETHING ELSE.
HEY... I'VE GOT AN IDEA!

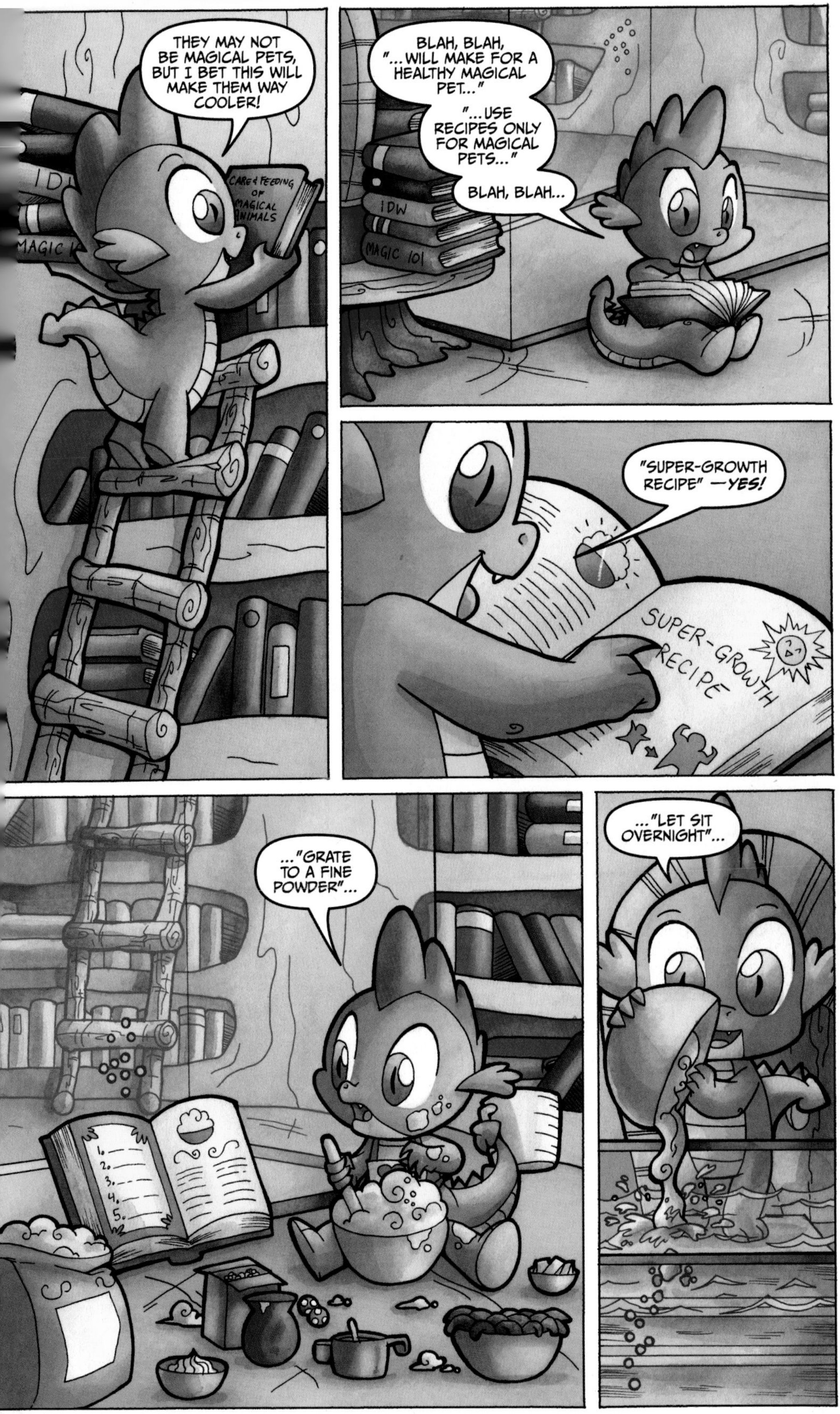
THEY MAY NOT BE MAGICAL PETS, BUT I BET THIS WILL MAKE THEM WAY COOLER!
CARE & FEEDING OF MAGICAL ANIMALS
IDW
MAGIC
BLAH, BLAH, "...WILL MAKE FOR A HEALTHY MAGICAL PET..."
"...USE RECIPES ONLY FOR MAGICAL PETS..."
BLAH, BLAH...
IDW
MAGIC 101
"SUPER-GROWTH RECIPE" —*YES!*
SUPER-GROWTH RECIPE
..."GRATE TO A FINE POWDER"...
..."LET SIT OVERNIGHT"...

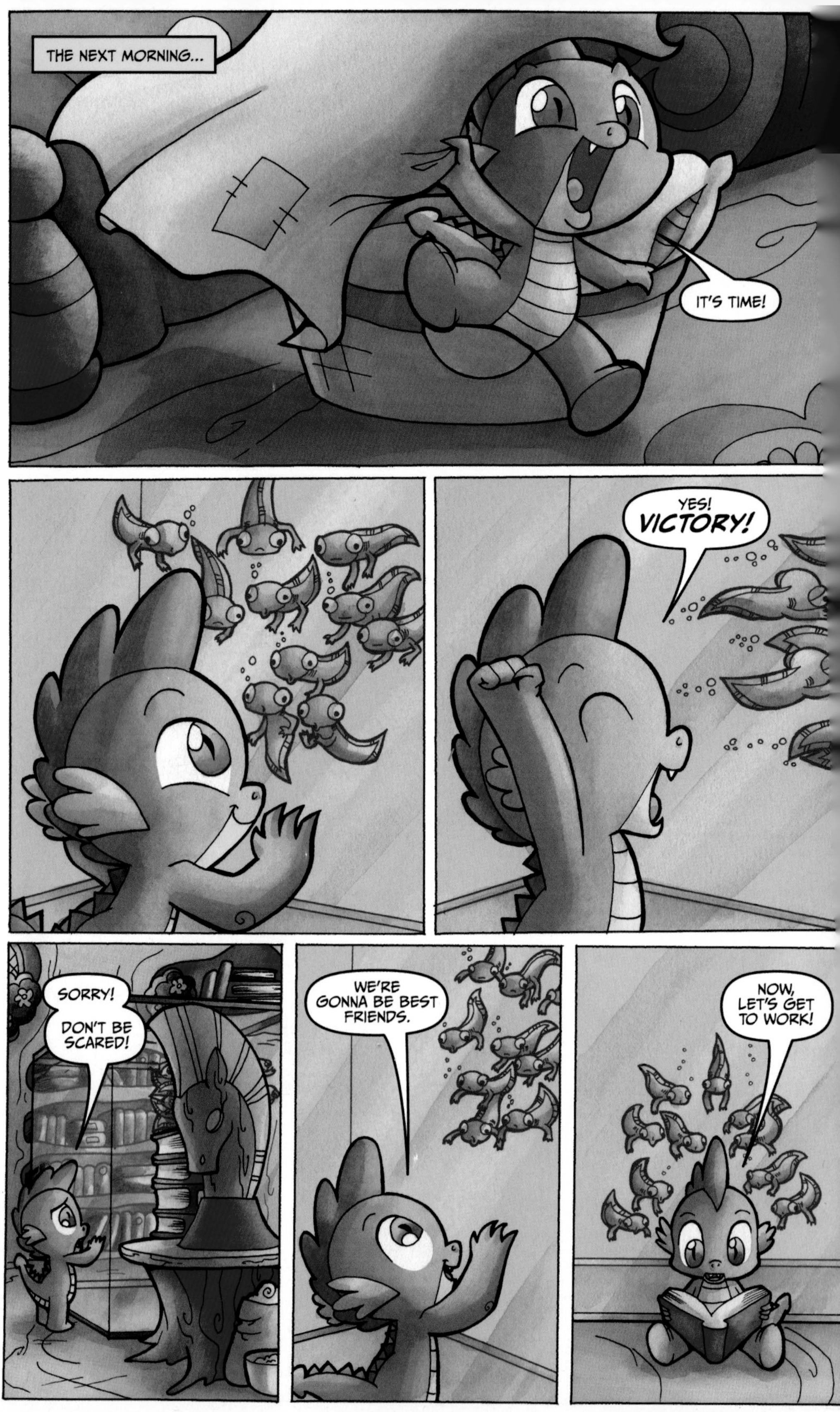
THE NEXT MORNING...
IT'S TIME!
YES! VICTORY!
SORRY!
DON'T BE SCARED!
WE'RE GONNA BE BEST FRIENDS.
NOW, LET'S GET TO WORK!

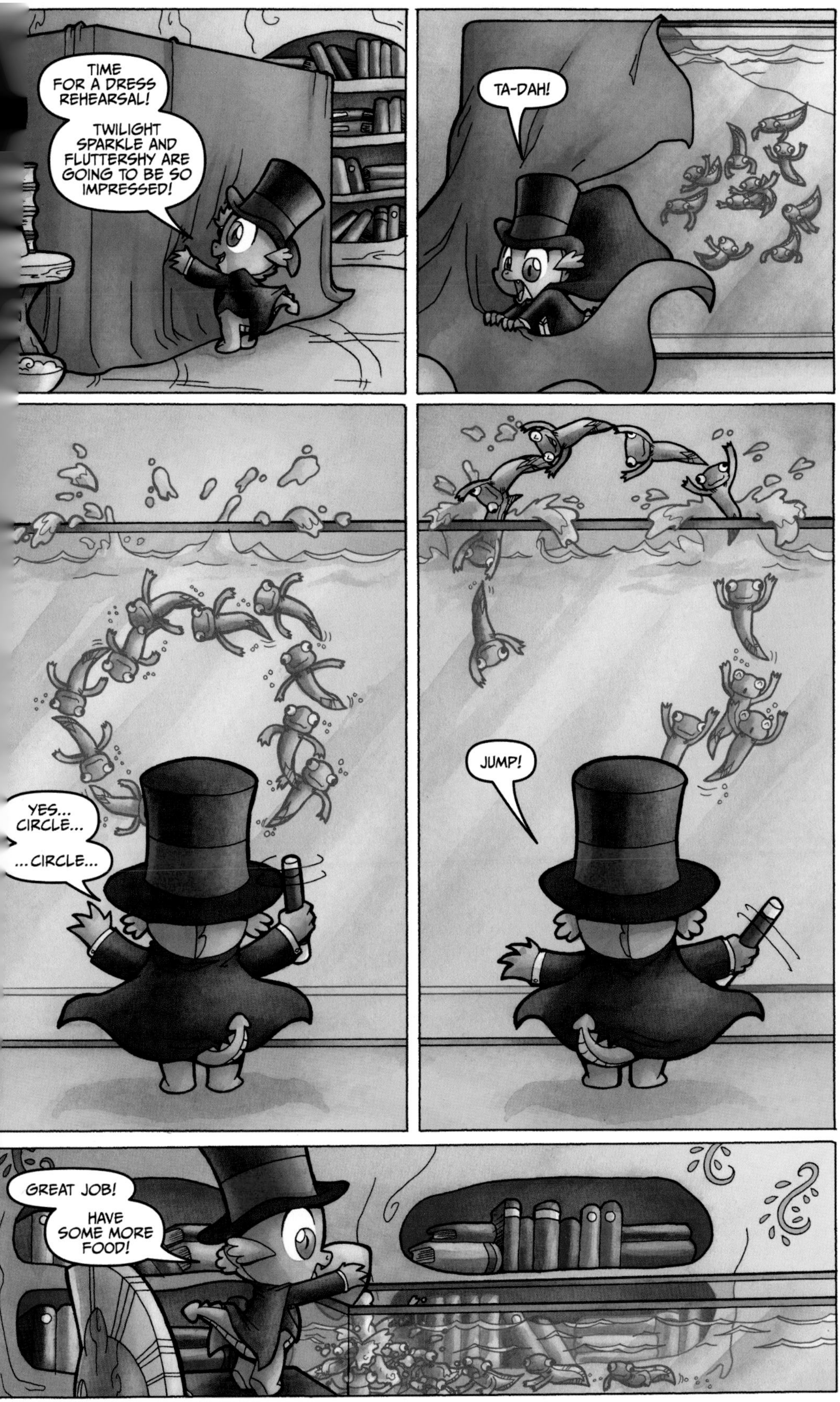
TIME FOR A DRESS REHEARSAL!
TWILIGHT SPARKLE AND FLUTTERSHY ARE GOING TO BE SO IMPRESSED!
TA-DAH!
YES... CIRCLE...
...CIRCLE...
JUMP!
GREAT JOB!
HAVE SOME MORE FOOD!

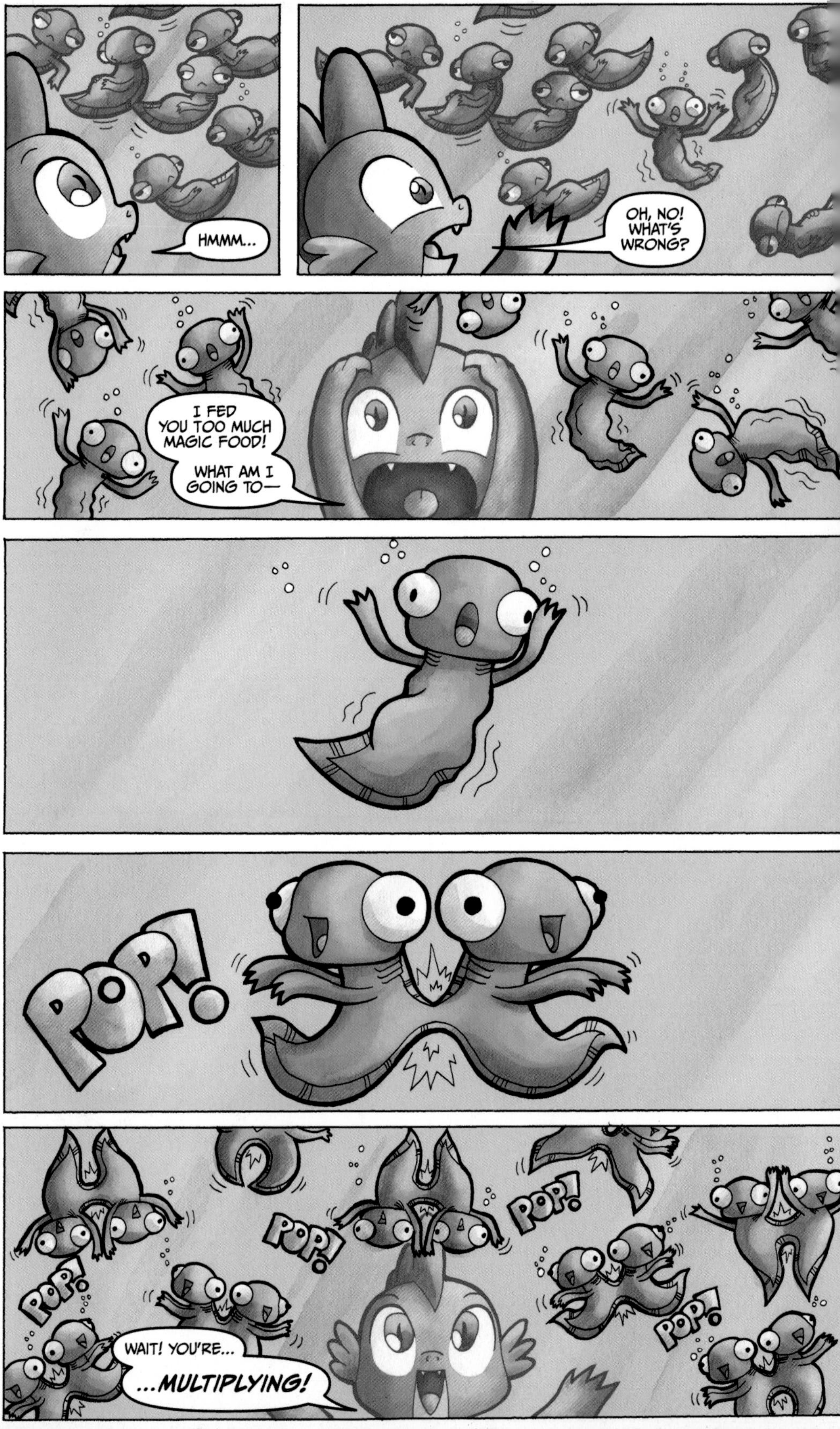
HMMM...
OH, NO! WHAT'S WRONG?
I FED YOU TOO MUCH MAGIC FOOD!
WHAT AM I GOING TO—
POP!
POP!
POP!
POP!
POP!
WAIT! YOU'RE...
...MULTIPLYING!

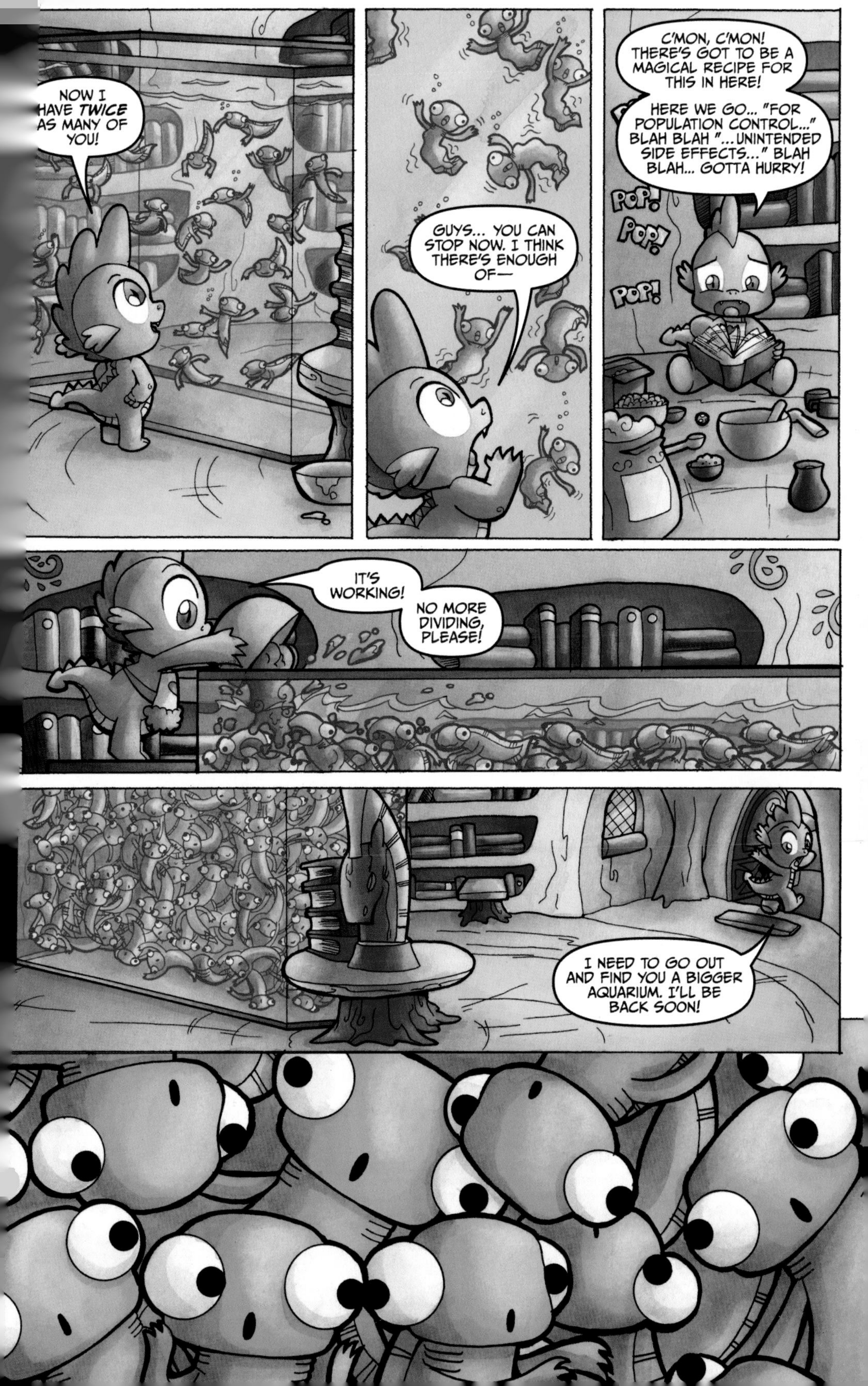
NOW I HAVE *TWICE* AS MANY OF YOU!
GUYS... YOU CAN STOP NOW. I THINK THERE'S ENOUGH OF—
C'MON, C'MON! THERE'S GOT TO BE A MAGICAL RECIPE FOR THIS IN HERE!
HERE WE GO... "FOR POPULATION CONTROL..." BLAH BLAH "...UNINTENDED SIDE EFFECTS..." BLAH BLAH... GOTTA HURRY!
POP!
POP!
POP!
IT'S WORKING!
NO MORE DIVIDING, PLEASE!
I NEED TO GO OUT AND FIND YOU A BIGGER AQUARIUM. I'LL BE BACK SOON!

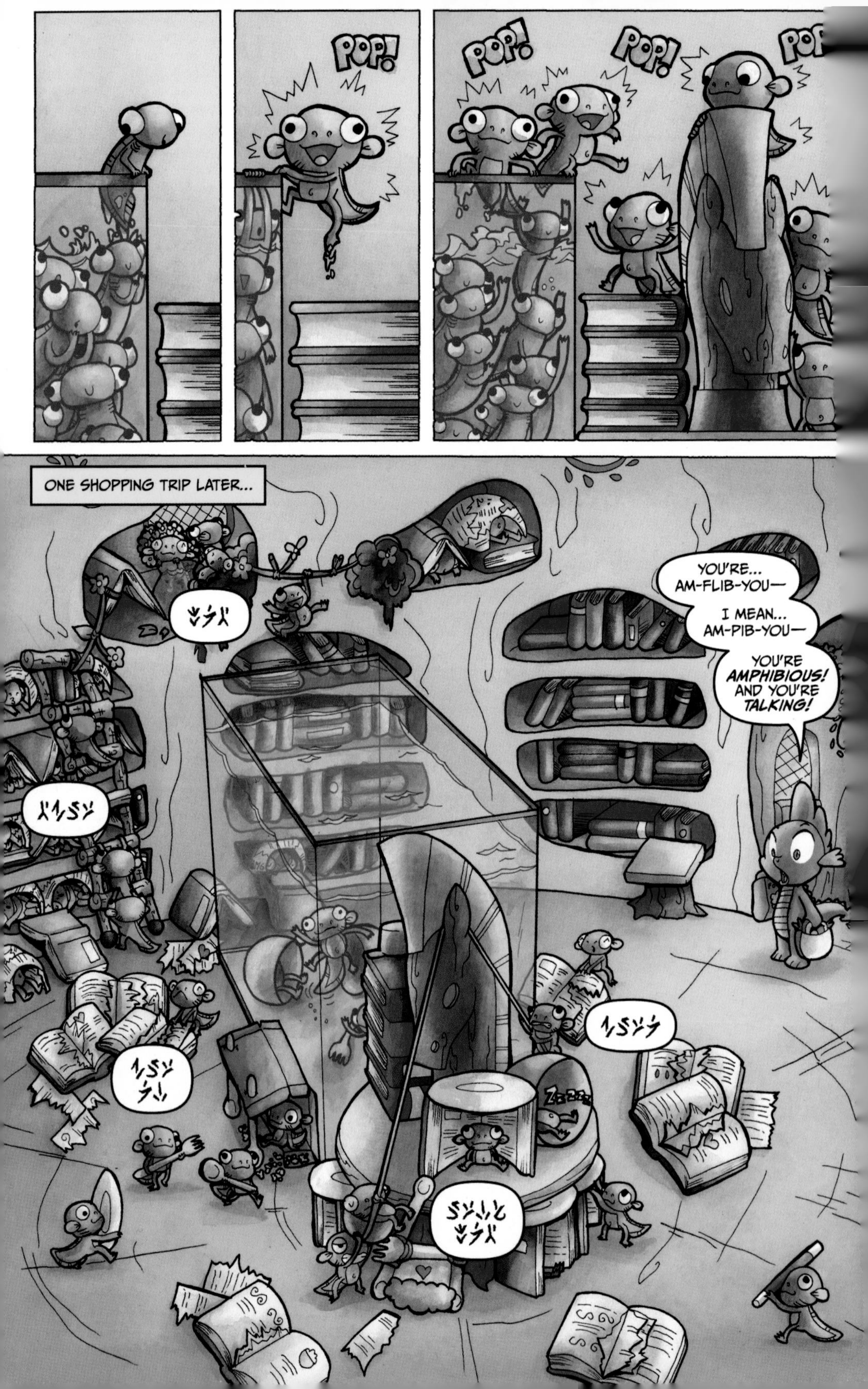
POP!
POP!
POP!
POP
ONE SHOPPING TRIP LATER...
YOU'RE... AM-FLIB-YOU—
I MEAN... AM-PIB-YOU—
YOU'RE *AMPHIBIOUS!* AND YOU'RE *TALKING!*
Zzzz

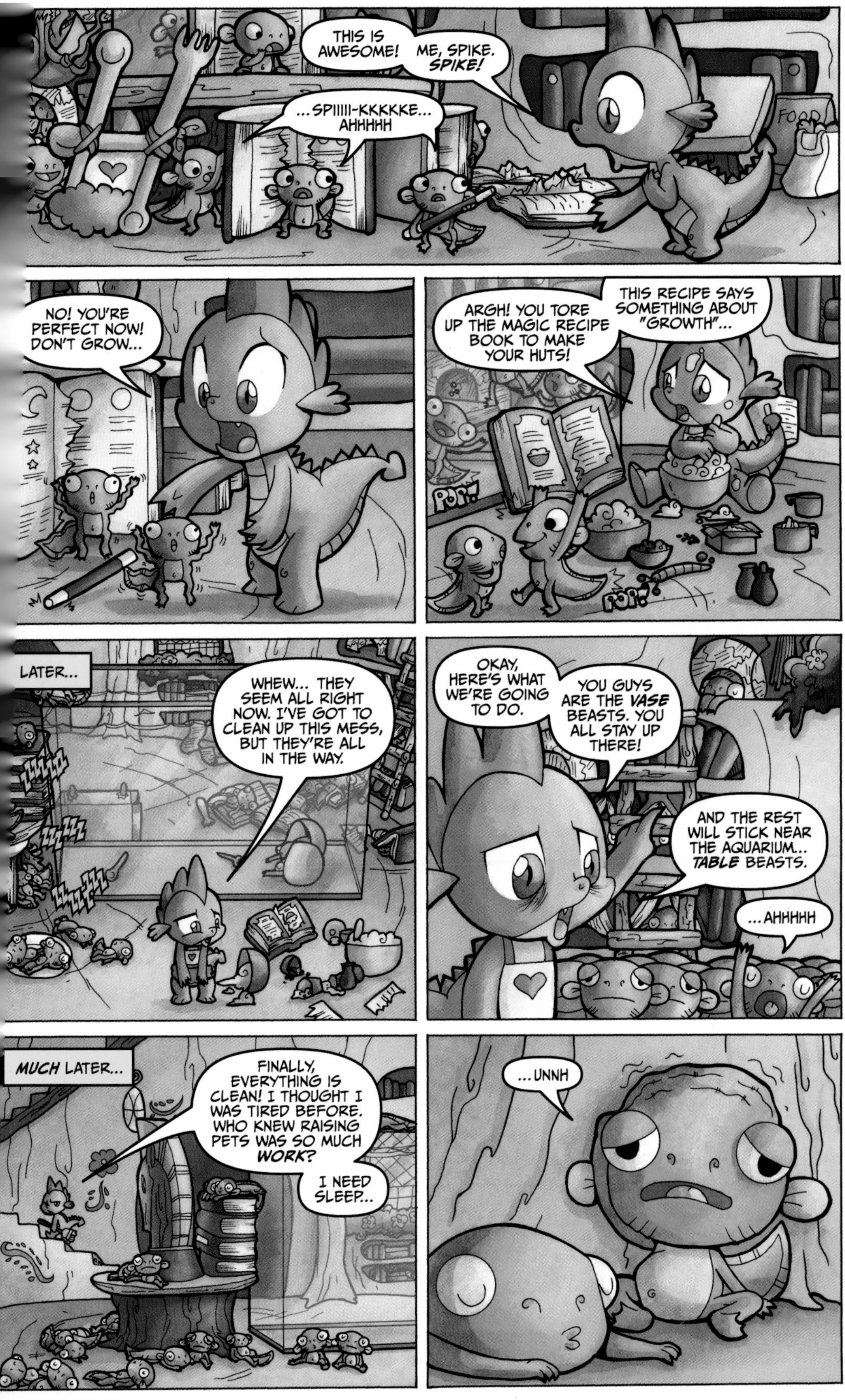
THIS IS AWESOME!
ME, SPIKE. *SPIKE!*
...SPIIIII-KKKKKE... AHHHHH
NO! YOU'RE PERFECT NOW! DON'T GROW...
ARGH! YOU TORE UP THE MAGIC RECIPE BOOK TO MAKE YOUR HUTS!
THIS RECIPE SAYS SOMETHING ABOUT "GROWTH"...
POP!
POP!
LATER...
WHEW... THEY SEEM ALL RIGHT NOW. I'VE GOT TO CLEAN UP THIS MESS, BUT THEY'RE ALL IN THE WAY.
OKAY, HERE'S WHAT WE'RE GOING TO DO.
YOU GUYS ARE THE *VASE* BEASTS. YOU ALL STAY UP THERE!
AND THE REST WILL STICK NEAR THE AQUARIUM... *TABLE* BEASTS.
...AHHHHH
MUCH LATER...
FINALLY, EVERYTHING IS CLEAN! I THOUGHT I WAS TIRED BEFORE. WHO KNEW RAISING PETS WAS SO MUCH *WORK*?
I NEED SLEEP...
...UNNH

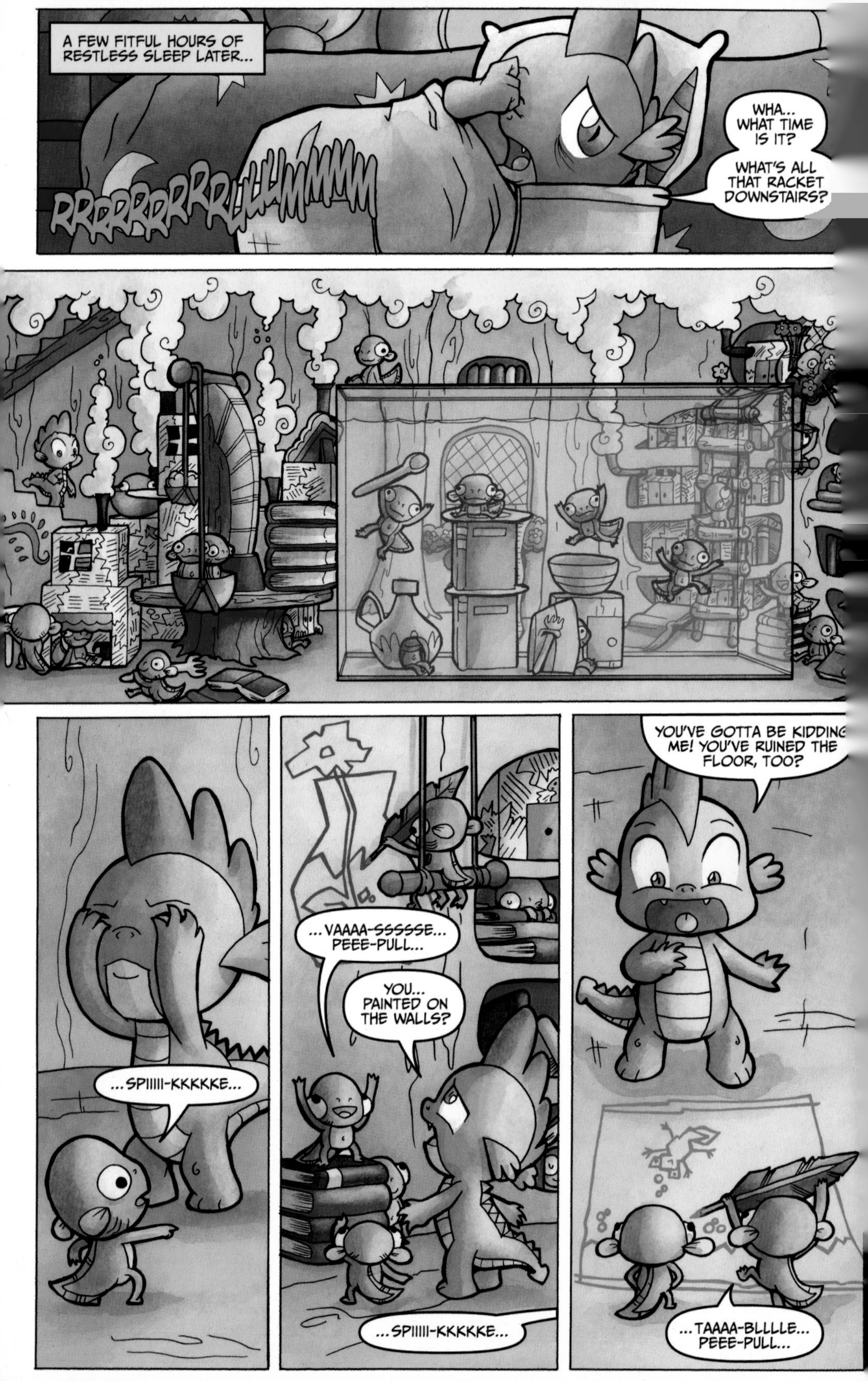
A FEW FITFUL HOURS OF RESTLESS SLEEP LATER...
RRRRRRRRRRUUMMMMM
WHA... WHAT TIME IS IT?
WHAT'S ALL THAT RACKET DOWNSTAIRS?
...SPIIIII-KKKKKE...
...VAAAA-SSSSSE... PEEE-PULL...
YOU... PAINTED ON THE WALLS?
...SPIIIII-KKKKKE...
YOU'VE GOTTA BE KIDDING ME! YOU'VE RUINED THE FLOOR, TOO?
...TAAAA-BLLLLE... PEEE-PULL...

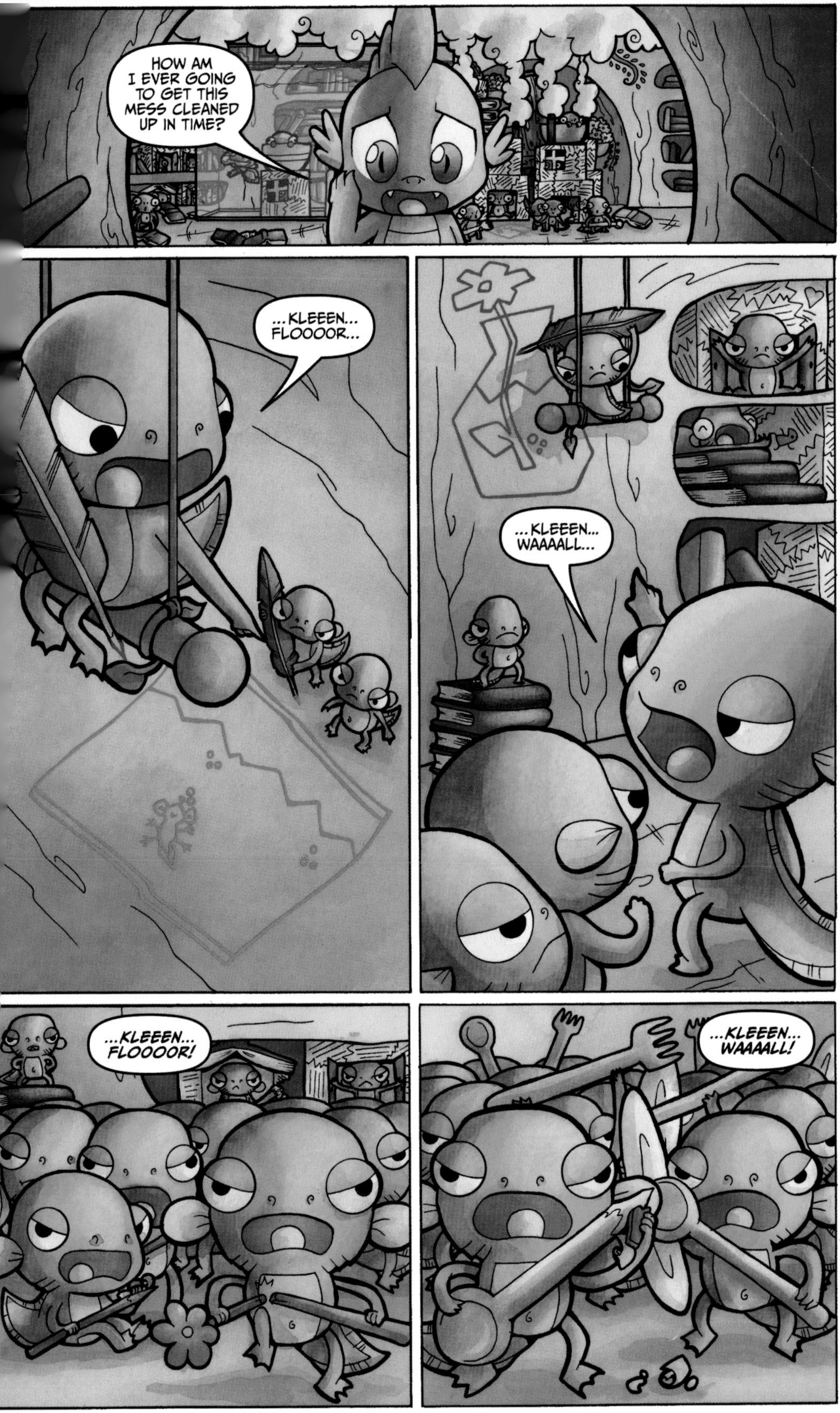

HOW AM I EVER GOING TO GET THIS MESS CLEANED UP IN TIME?
...KLEEEN... FLOOOOR...
...KLEEEN... WAAAALL...
...KLEEEN... FLOOOOR!
...KLEEEN... WAAAALL!

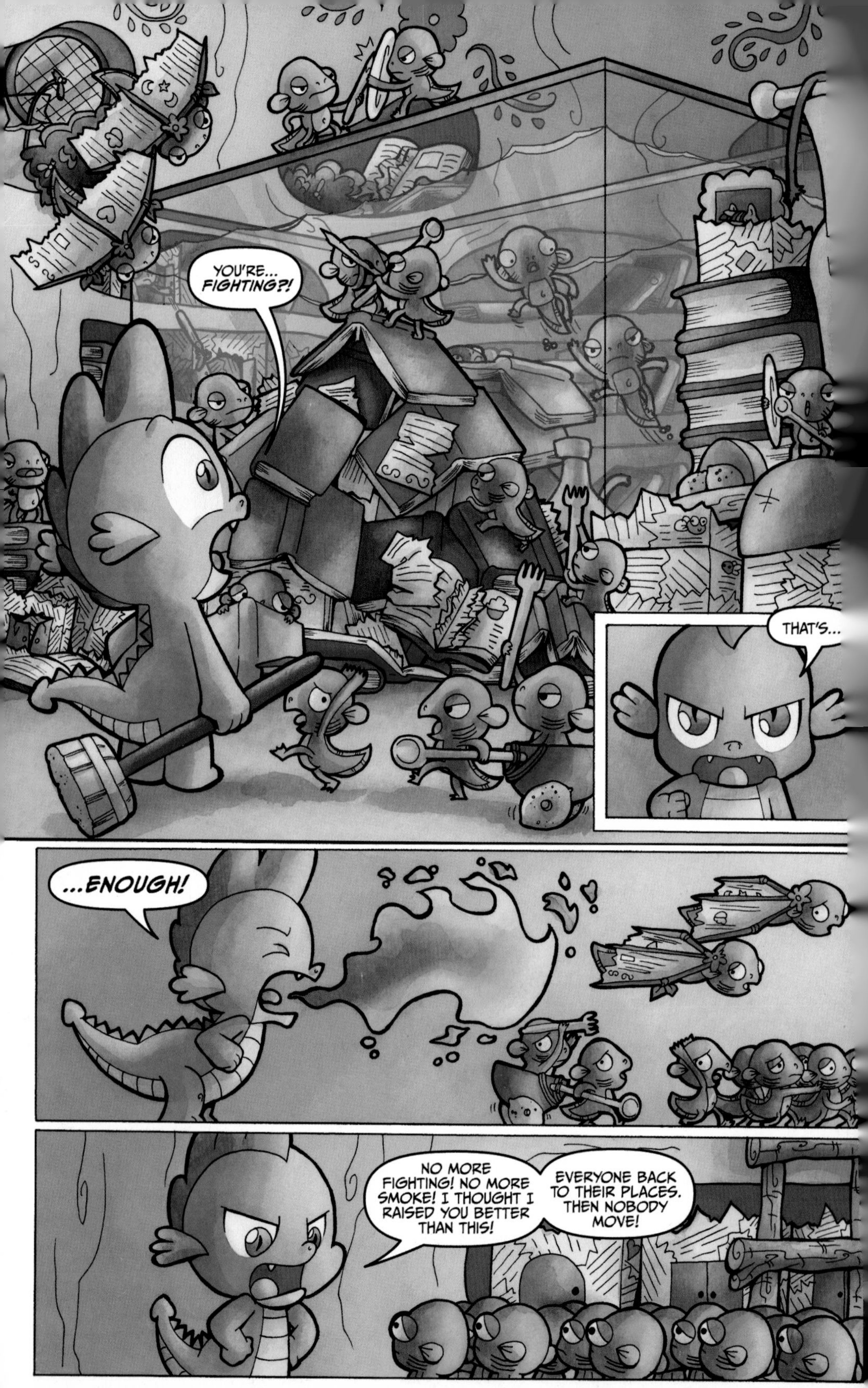
YOU'RE... FIGHTING?!
THAT'S...
...ENOUGH!
NO MORE FIGHTING! NO MORE SMOKE! I THOUGHT I RAISED YOU BETTER THAN THIS!
EVERYONE BACK TO THEIR PLACES. THEN NOBODY MOVE!

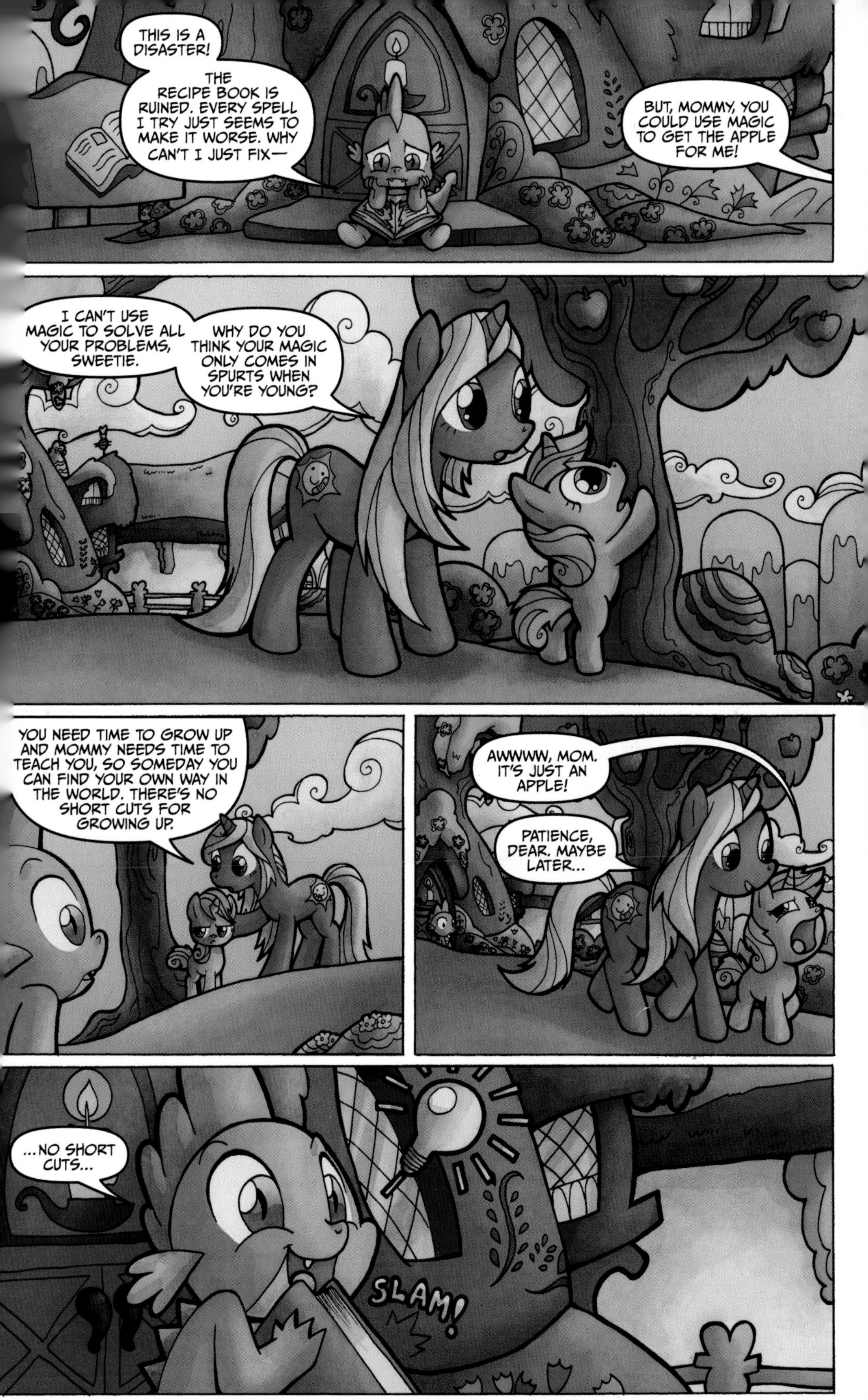
THIS IS A DISASTER!
THE RECIPE BOOK IS RUINED. EVERY SPELL I TRY JUST SEEMS TO MAKE IT WORSE. WHY CAN'T I JUST FIX—
BUT, MOMMY, YOU COULD USE MAGIC TO GET THE APPLE FOR ME!
I CAN'T USE MAGIC TO SOLVE ALL YOUR PROBLEMS, SWEETIE.
WHY DO YOU THINK YOUR MAGIC ONLY COMES IN SPURTS WHEN YOU'RE YOUNG?
YOU NEED TIME TO GROW UP AND MOMMY NEEDS TIME TO TEACH YOU, SO SOMEDAY YOU CAN FIND YOUR OWN WAY IN THE WORLD. THERE'S NO SHORT CUTS FOR GROWING UP.
AWWWW, MOM. IT'S JUST AN APPLE!
PATIENCE, DEAR. MAYBE LATER...
...NO SHORT CUTS...
SLAM!

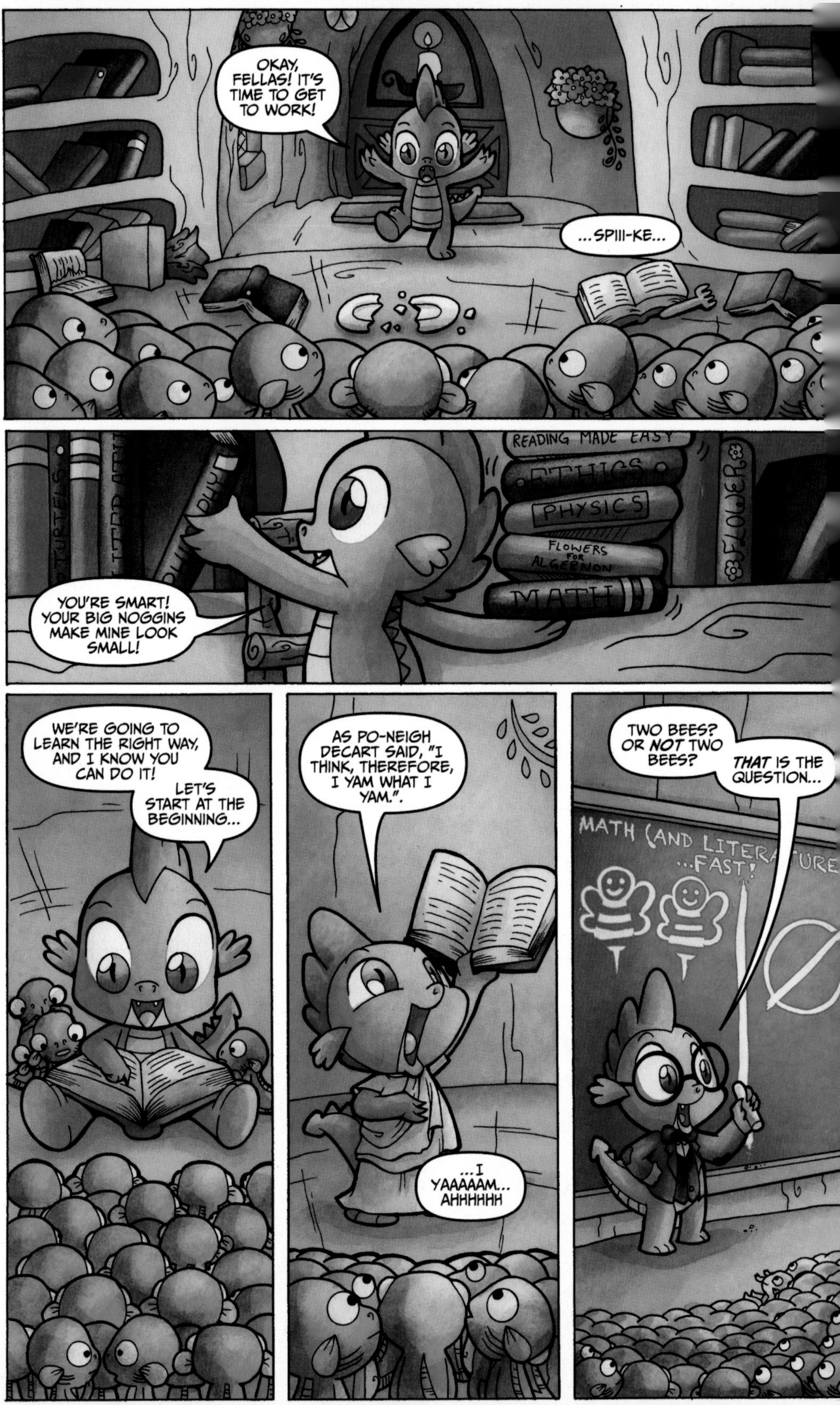
OKAY, FELLAS! IT'S TIME TO GET TO WORK!
...SPIII-KE...
READING MADE EASY
ETHICS
PHYSICS
FLOWERS FOR ALGERNON
MATH
YOU'RE SMART! YOUR BIG NOGGINS MAKE MINE LOOK SMALL!
WE'RE GOING TO LEARN THE RIGHT WAY, AND I KNOW YOU CAN DO IT!
LET'S START AT THE BEGINNING...
AS PO-NEIGH DECART SAID, "I THINK, THEREFORE, I YAM WHAT I YAM.".
...I YAAAAAM... AHHHHHH
TWO BEES? OR NOT TWO BEES?
THAT IS THE QUESTION...
MATH (AND LITERATURE ...FAST!

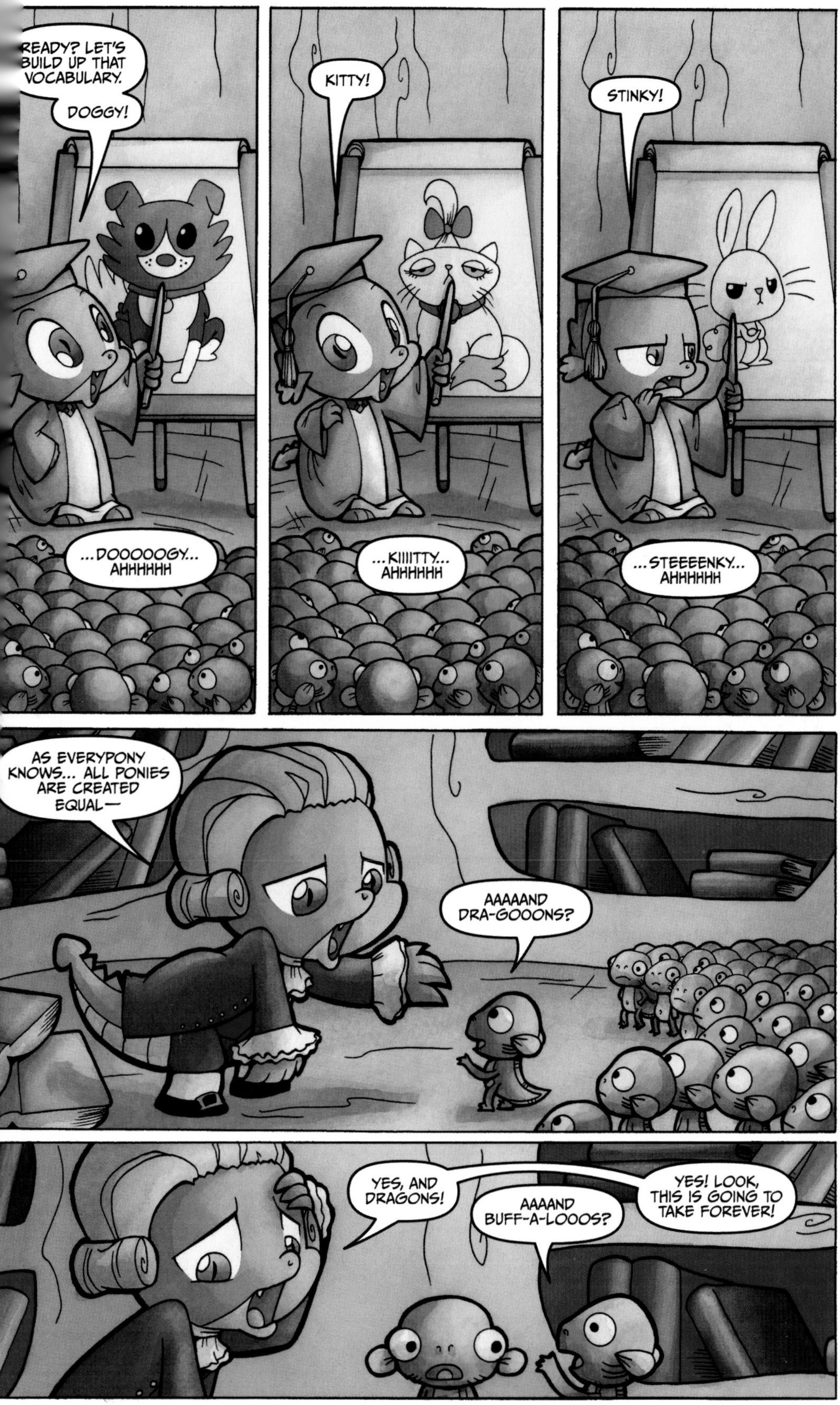
READY? LET'S BUILD UP THAT VOCABULARY.
DOGGY!
...DOOOOOGY... AHHHHHH
KITTY!
...KIIIITTY... AHHHHHH
STINKY!
...STEEEENKY... AHHHHHH
AS EVERYPONY KNOWS... ALL PONIES ARE CREATED EQUAL—
AAAAAND DRA-GOOONS?
YES, AND DRAGONS!
AAAAND BUFF-A-LOOOS?
YES! LOOK, THIS IS GOING TO TAKE FOREVER!

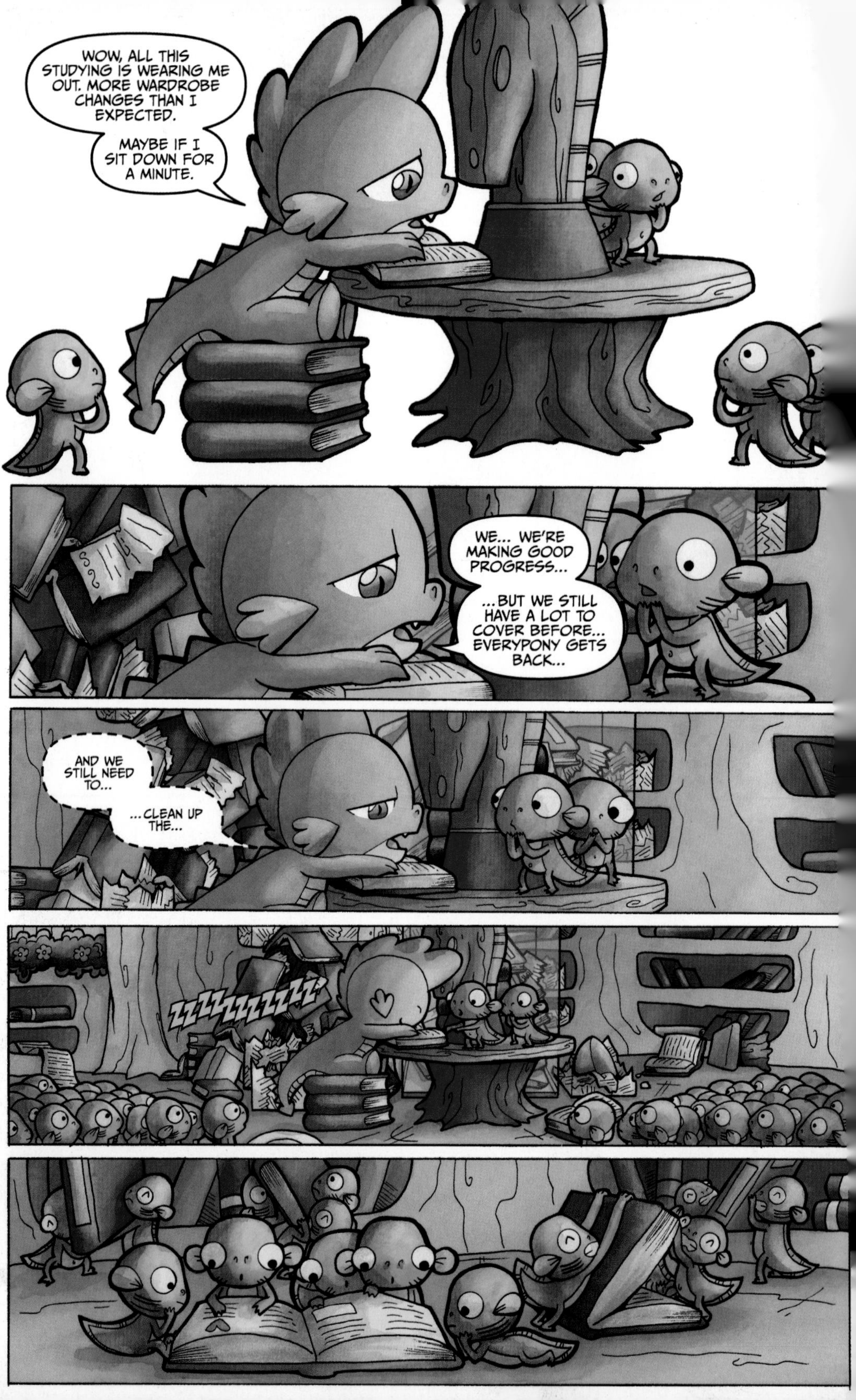
WOW, ALL THIS STUDYING IS WEARING ME OUT. MORE WARDROBE CHANGES THAN I EXPECTED.
MAYBE IF I SIT DOWN FOR A MINUTE.
WE... WE'RE MAKING GOOD PROGRESS...
...BUT WE STILL HAVE A LOT TO COVER BEFORE... EVERYPONY GETS BACK...
AND WE STILL NEED TO...
...CLEAN UP THE...
ZZZZZZZZZZZZ

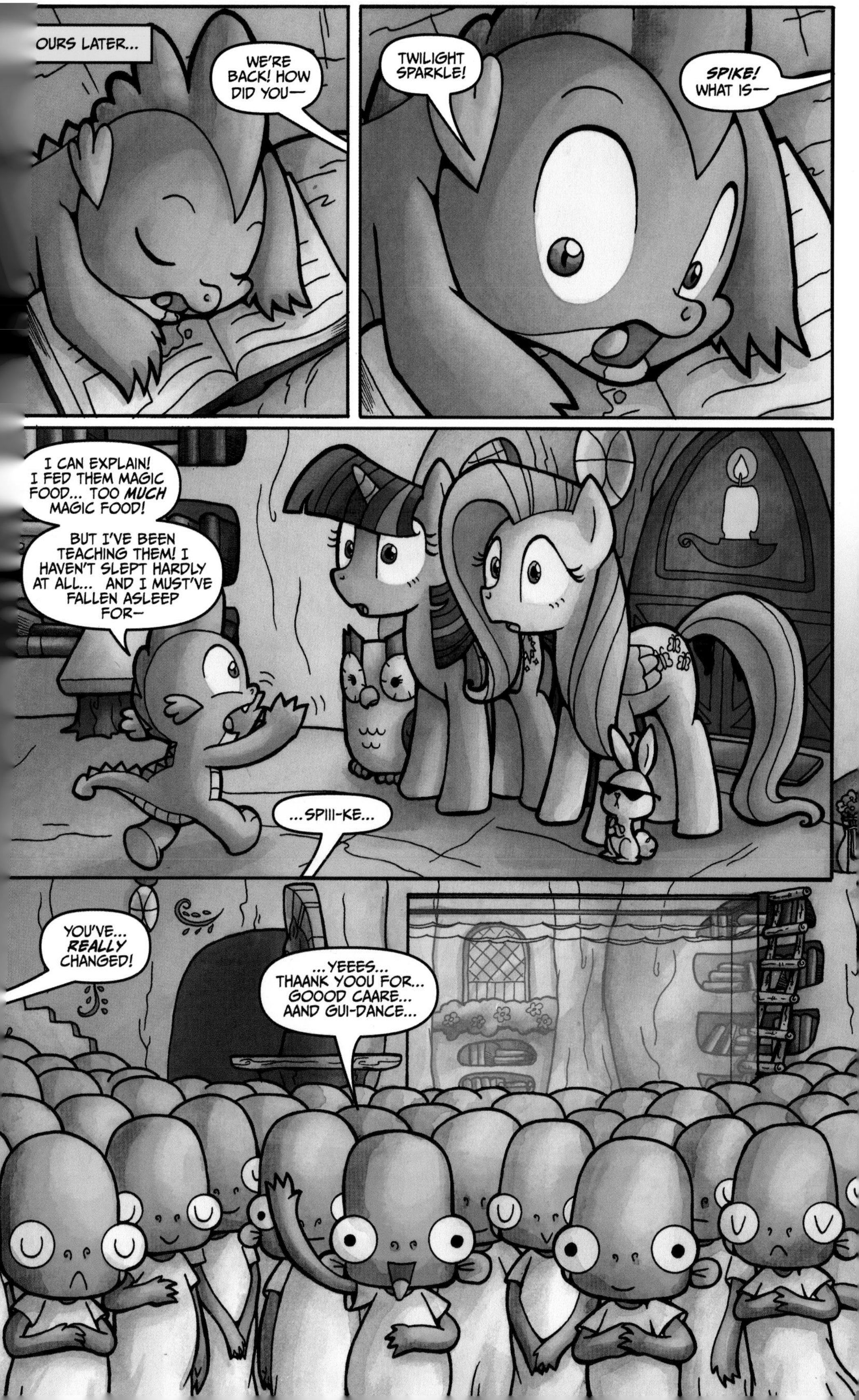
OURS LATER...
WE'RE BACK! HOW DID YOU—
TWILIGHT SPARKLE!
SPIKE! WHAT IS—
I CAN EXPLAIN! I FED THEM MAGIC FOOD... TOO MUCH MAGIC FOOD!
BUT I'VE BEEN TEACHING THEM! I HAVEN'T SLEPT HARDLY AT ALL... AND I MUST'VE FALLEN ASLEEP FOR—
...SPIII-KE...
YOU'VE... REALLY CHANGED!
...YEEES... THAANK YOOU FOR... GOOOD CAARE... AAND GUI-DANCE...

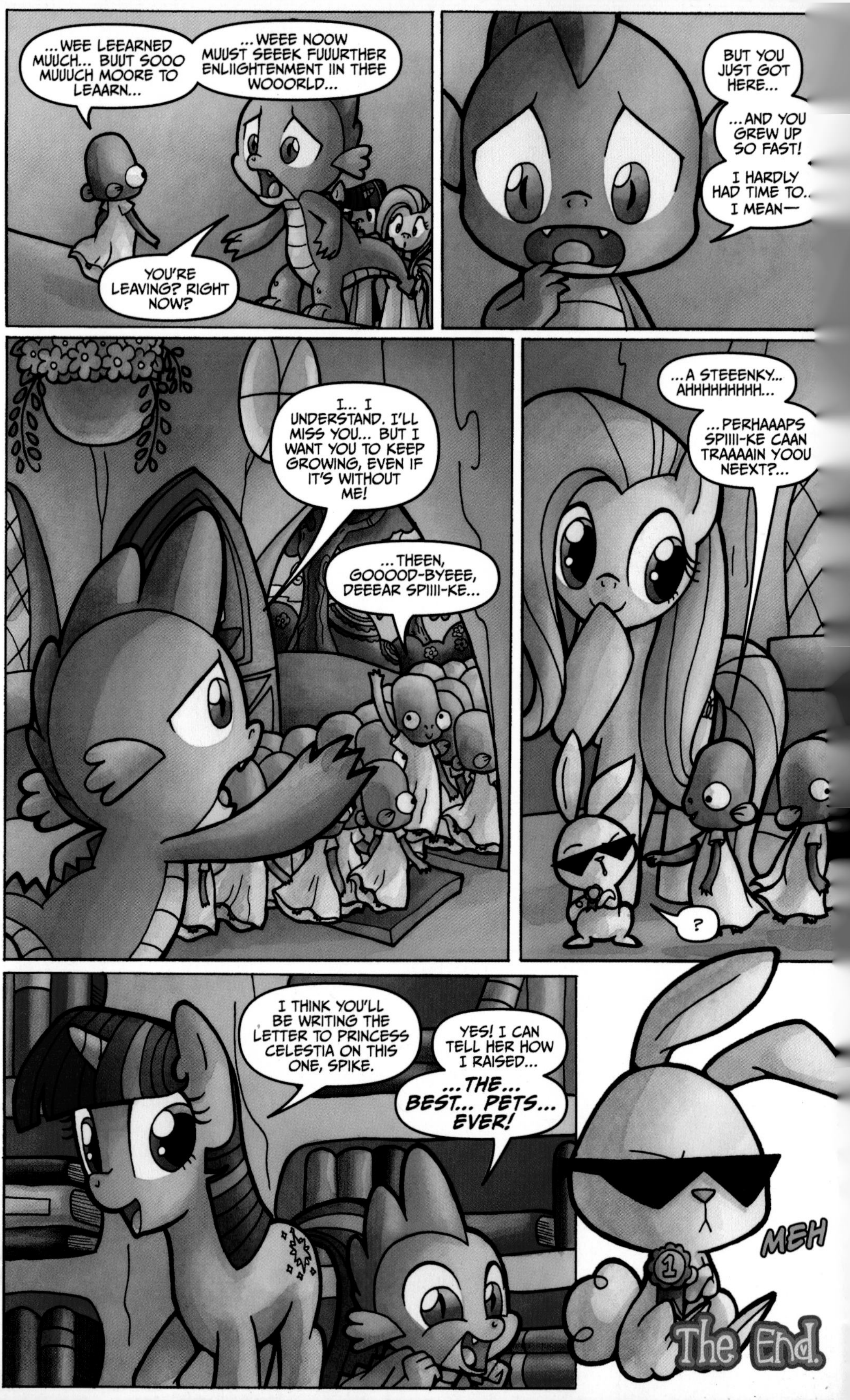
...WEE LEEARNED MUUCH... BUUT SOOO MUUUCH MOORE TO LEAARN...
...WEEE NOOW MUUST SEEEK FUUURTHER ENLIIGHTENMENT IIN THEE WOOORLD...
YOU'RE LEAVING? RIGHT NOW?
BUT YOU JUST GOT HERE...
...AND YOU GREW UP SO FAST!
I HARDLY HAD TIME TO... I MEAN—
I... I UNDERSTAND. I'LL MISS YOU... BUT I WANT YOU TO KEEP GROWING, EVEN IF IT'S WITHOUT ME!
...THEEN, GOOOOD-BYEEE, DEEEAR SPIIII-KE...
...A STEEENKY... AHHHHHHHHH...
...PERHAAAPS SPIIII-KE CAAN TRAAAAIN YOOU NEEXT?...
?
I THINK YOU'LL BE WRITING THE LETTER TO PRINCESS CELESTIA ON THIS ONE, SPIKE.
YES! I CAN TELL HER HOW I RAISED...
...THE... BEST... PETS... EVER!
MEH
The End.

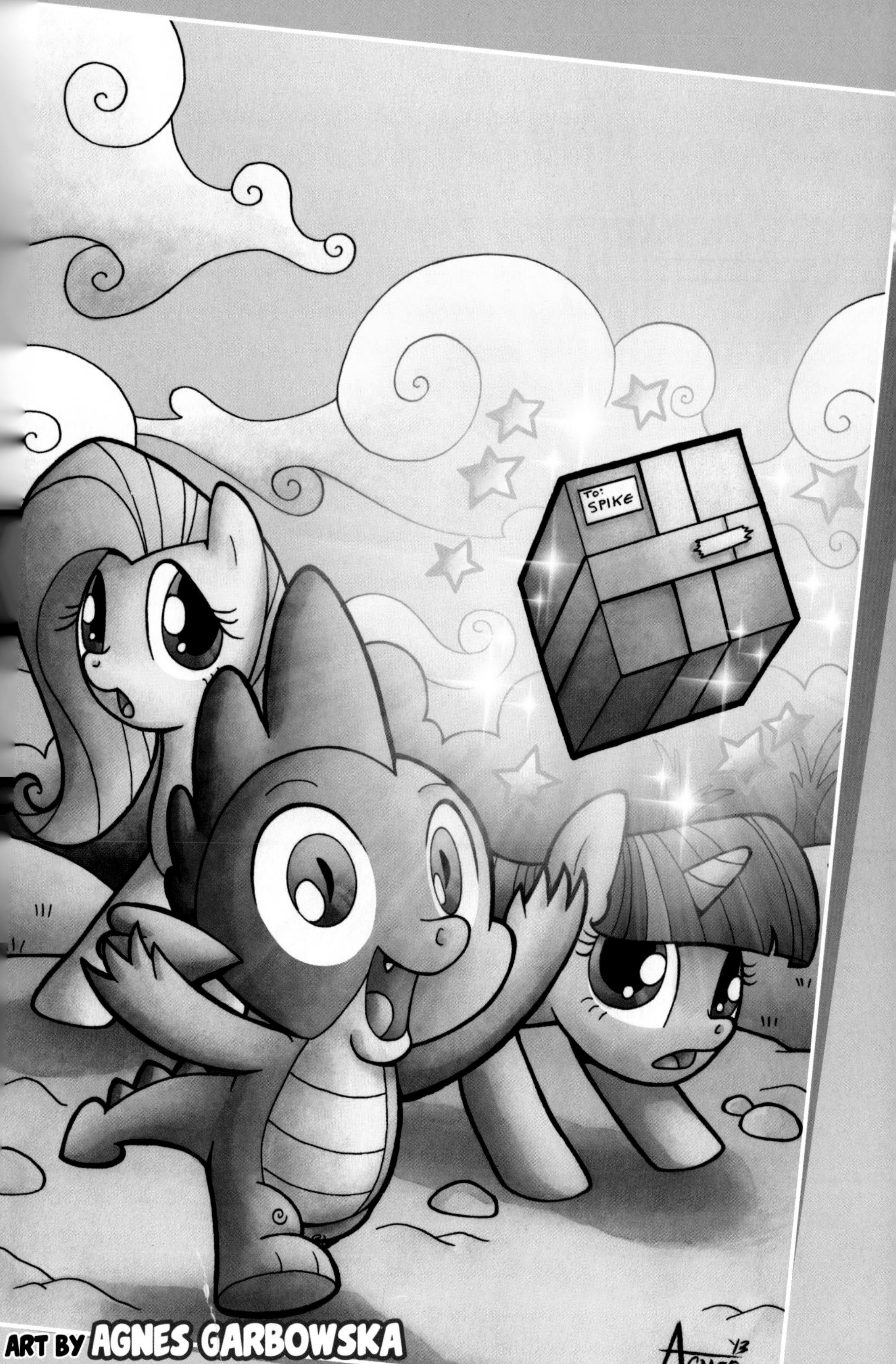
To: SPIKE
AGNES '13

ART BY AGNES GARBOWSKA

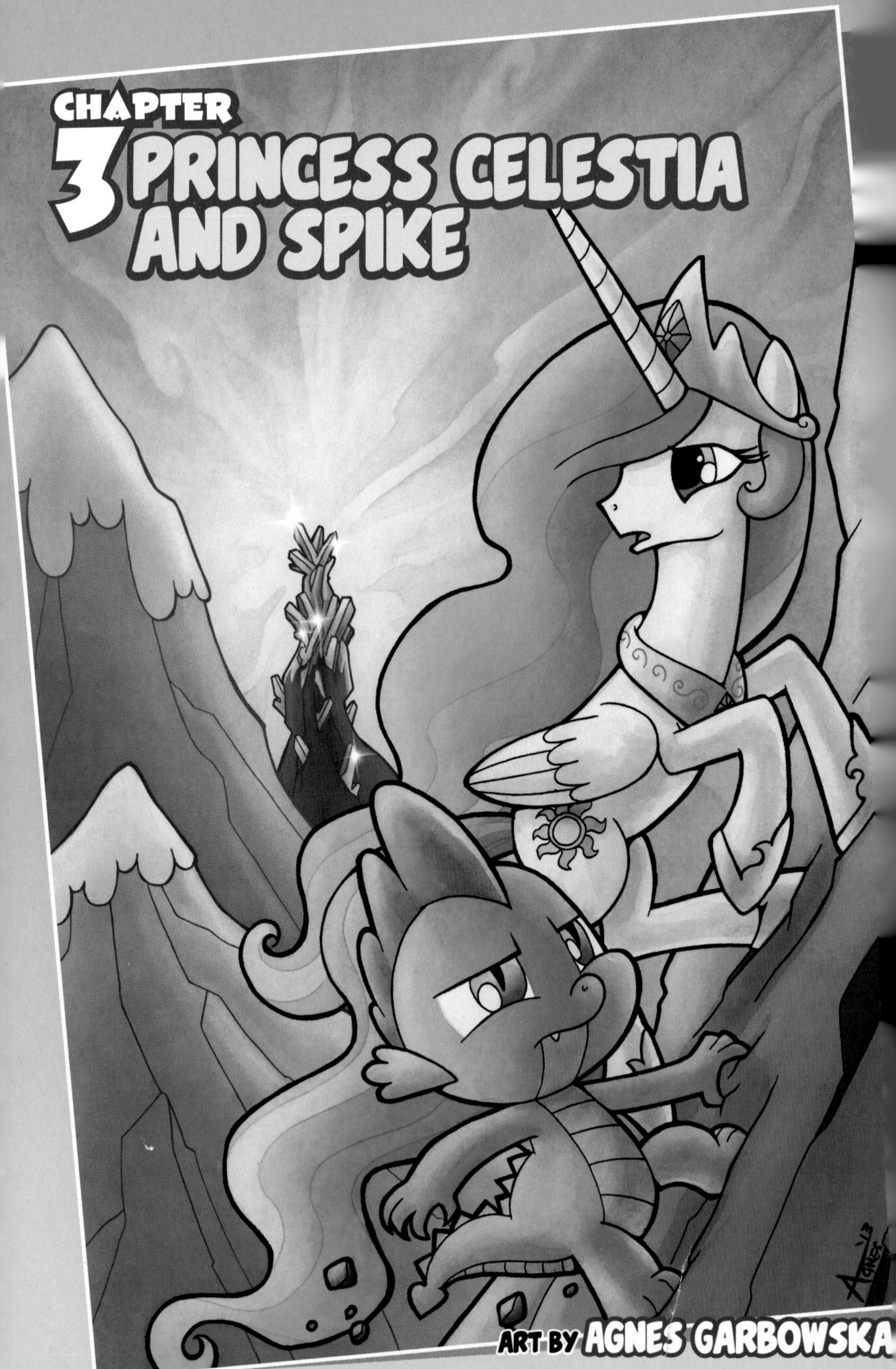
CHAPTER 3
PRINCESS CELESTIA AND SPIKE
ART BY AGNES GARBOWSKA

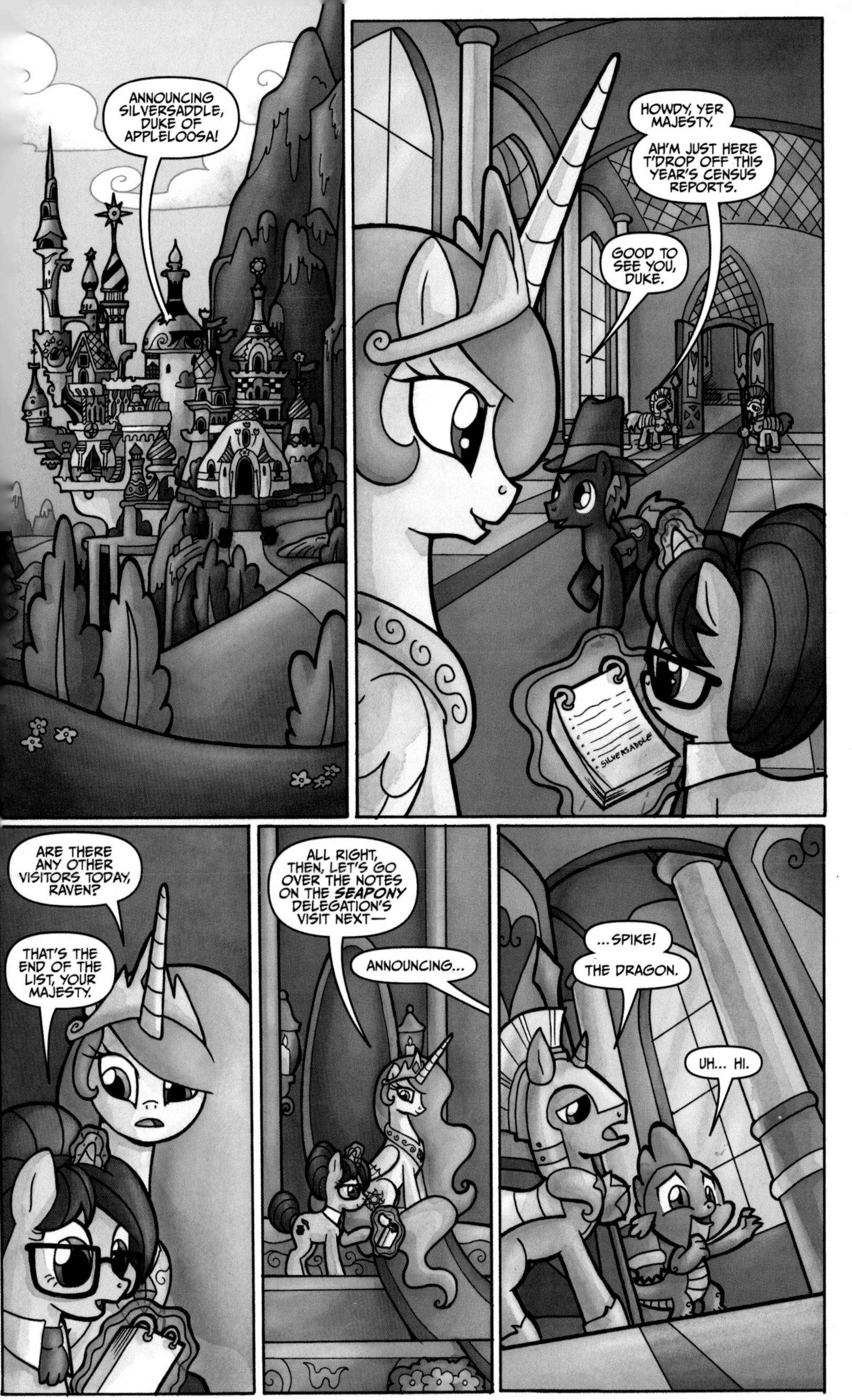
ANNOUNCING SILVERSADDLE, DUKE OF APPLELOOSA!
HOWDY, YER MAJESTY.
AH'M JUST HERE T'DROP OFF THIS YEAR'S CENSUS REPORTS.
GOOD TO SEE YOU, DUKE.
SILVERSADDLE
ARE THERE ANY OTHER VISITORS TODAY, RAVEN?
THAT'S THE END OF THE LIST, YOUR MAJESTY.
ALL RIGHT, THEN, LET'S GO OVER THE NOTES ON THE SEAPONY DELEGATION'S VISIT NEXT—
ANNOUNCING...
...SPIKE!
THE DRAGON.
UH... HI.

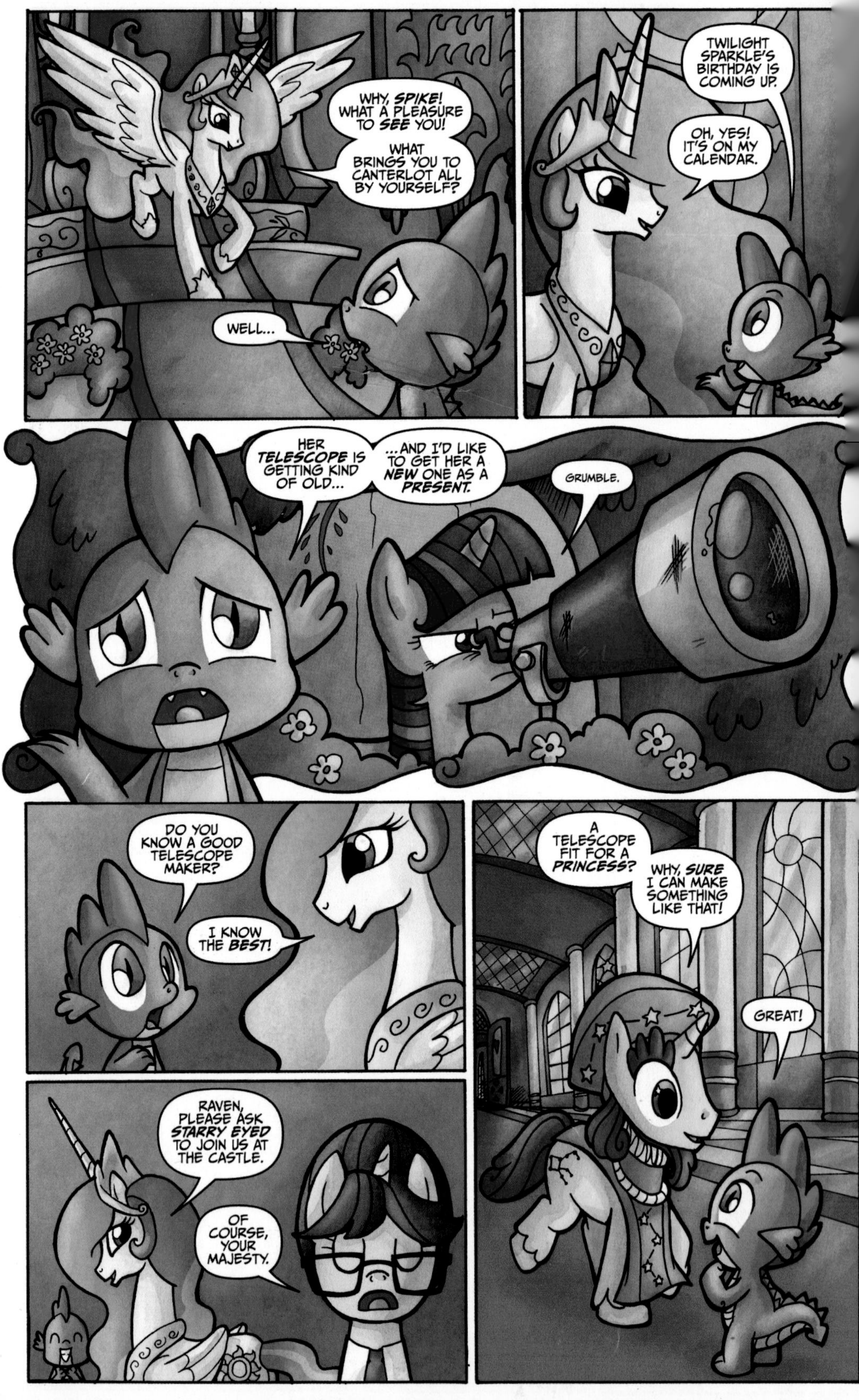
WHY, SPIKE! WHAT A PLEASURE TO SEE YOU!
WHAT BRINGS YOU TO CANTERLOT ALL BY YOURSELF?
WELL...
TWILIGHT SPARKLE'S BIRTHDAY IS COMING UP.
OH, YES! IT'S ON MY CALENDAR.
HER TELESCOPE IS GETTING KIND OF OLD...
...AND I'D LIKE TO GET HER A NEW ONE AS A PRESENT.
GRUMBLE.
DO YOU KNOW A GOOD TELESCOPE MAKER?
I KNOW THE BEST!
RAVEN, PLEASE ASK STARRY EYED TO JOIN US AT THE CASTLE.
OF COURSE, YOUR MAJESTY.
A TELESCOPE FIT FOR A PRINCESS?
WHY, SURE I CAN MAKE SOMETHING LIKE THAT!
GREAT!

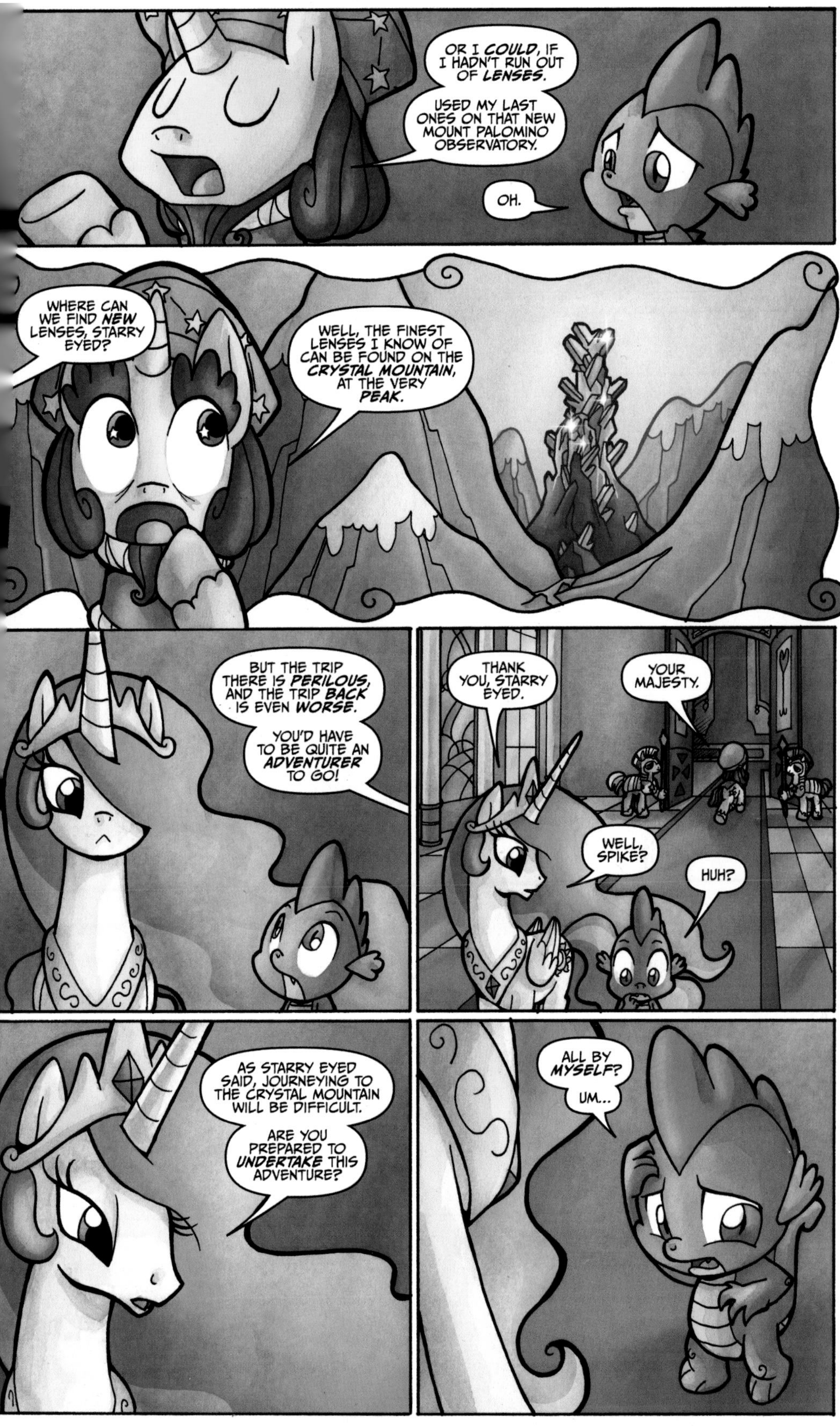

OR I *COULD*, IF I HADN'T RUN OUT OF *LENSES*.
USED MY LAST ONES ON THAT NEW MOUNT PALOMINO OBSERVATORY.
OH.
WHERE CAN WE FIND *NEW* LENSES, STARRY EYED?
WELL, THE FINEST LENSES I KNOW OF CAN BE FOUND ON THE *CRYSTAL MOUNTAIN*, AT THE VERY *PEAK*.
BUT THE TRIP THERE IS *PERILOUS*, AND THE TRIP *BACK* IS EVEN *WORSE*.
YOU'D HAVE TO BE QUITE AN *ADVENTURER* TO GO!
THANK YOU, STARRY EYED.
YOUR MAJESTY.
WELL, SPIKE?
HUH?
AS STARRY EYED SAID, JOURNEYING TO THE CRYSTAL MOUNTAIN WILL BE DIFFICULT.
ARE YOU PREPARED TO *UNDERTAKE* THIS ADVENTURE?
ALL BY *MYSELF*?
UM...

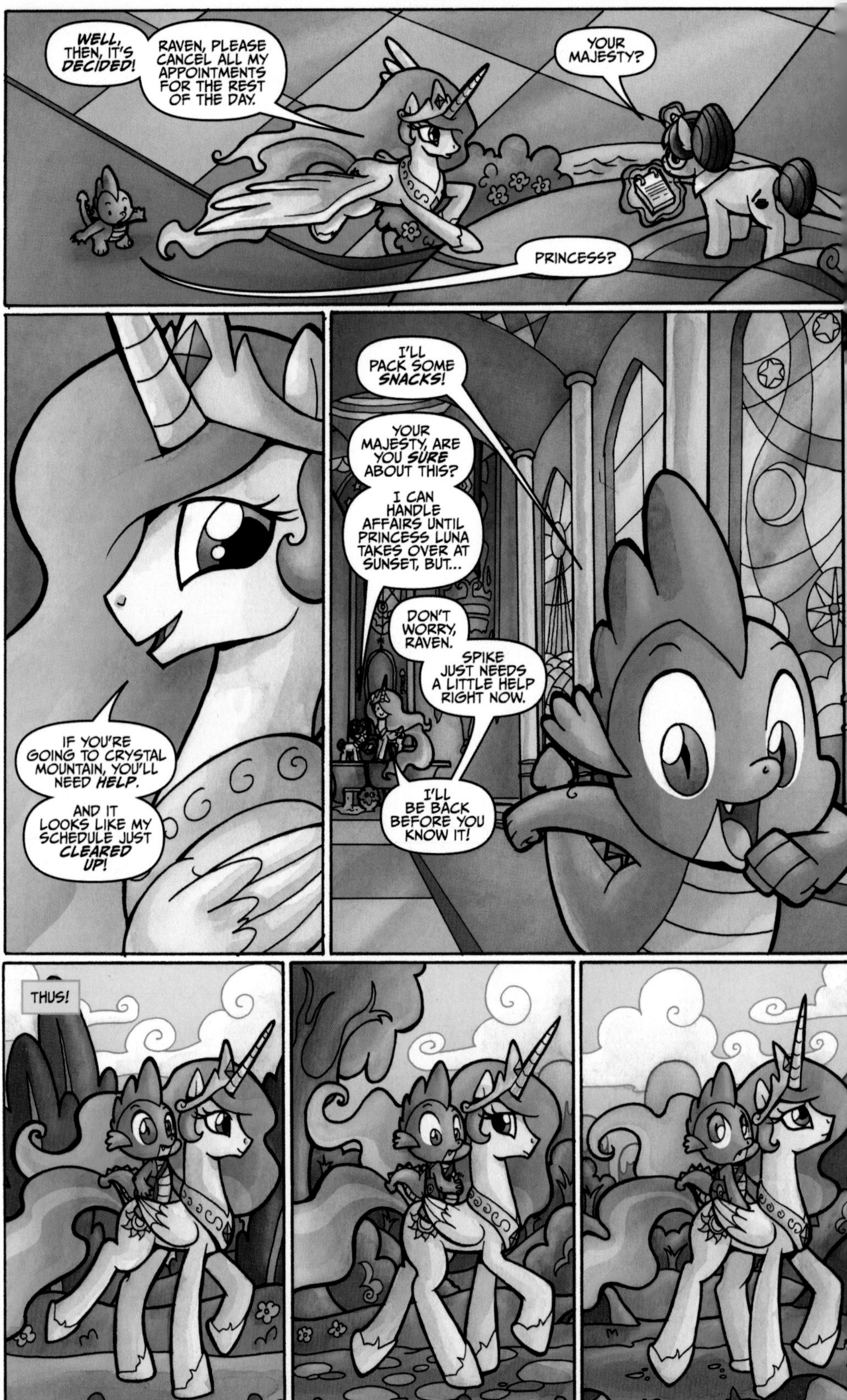
WELL, THEN, IT'S DECIDED!
RAVEN, PLEASE CANCEL ALL MY APPOINTMENTS FOR THE REST OF THE DAY.
YOUR MAJESTY?
PRINCESS?
IF YOU'RE GOING TO CRYSTAL MOUNTAIN, YOU'LL NEED HELP.
AND IT LOOKS LIKE MY SCHEDULE JUST CLEARED UP!
I'LL PACK SOME SNACKS!
YOUR MAJESTY, ARE YOU SURE ABOUT THIS?
I CAN HANDLE AFFAIRS UNTIL PRINCESS LUNA TAKES OVER AT SUNSET, BUT...
DON'T WORRY, RAVEN.
SPIKE JUST NEEDS A LITTLE HELP RIGHT NOW.
I'LL BE BACK BEFORE YOU KNOW IT!
THUS!

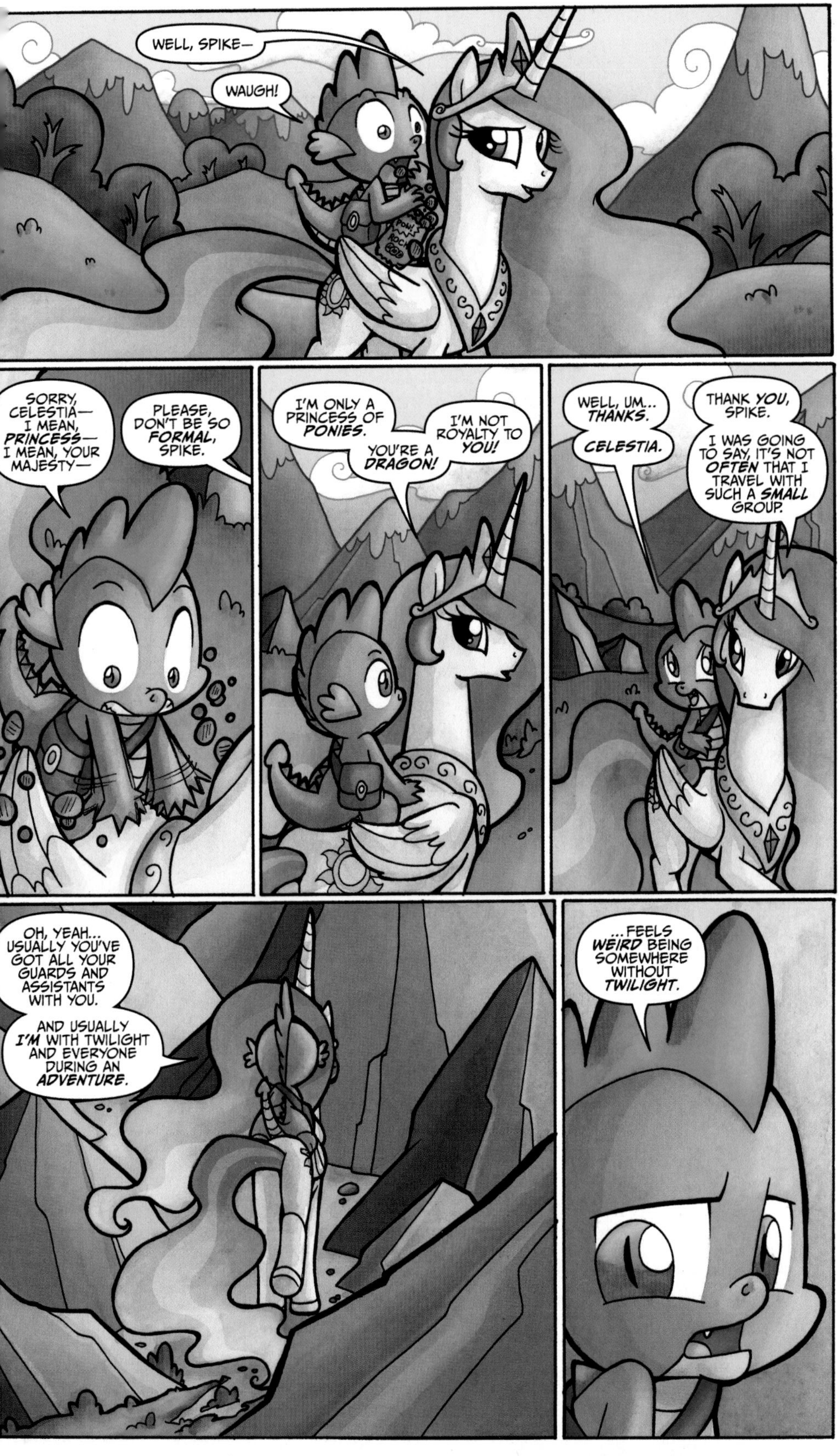
WELL, SPIKE—
WAUGH!
SORRY, CELESTIA— I MEAN, PRINCESS— I MEAN, YOUR MAJESTY—
PLEASE, DON'T BE SO FORMAL, SPIKE.
I'M ONLY A PRINCESS OF PONIES.
I'M NOT ROYALTY TO YOU!
YOU'RE A DRAGON!
WELL, UM... THANKS.
CELESTIA.
THANK YOU, SPIKE.
I WAS GOING TO SAY, IT'S NOT OFTEN THAT I TRAVEL WITH SUCH A SMALL GROUP.
OH, YEAH... USUALLY YOU'VE GOT ALL YOUR GUARDS AND ASSISTANTS WITH YOU.
AND USUALLY I'M WITH TWILIGHT AND EVERYONE DURING AN ADVENTURE.
...FEELS WEIRD BEING SOMEWHERE WITHOUT TWILIGHT.

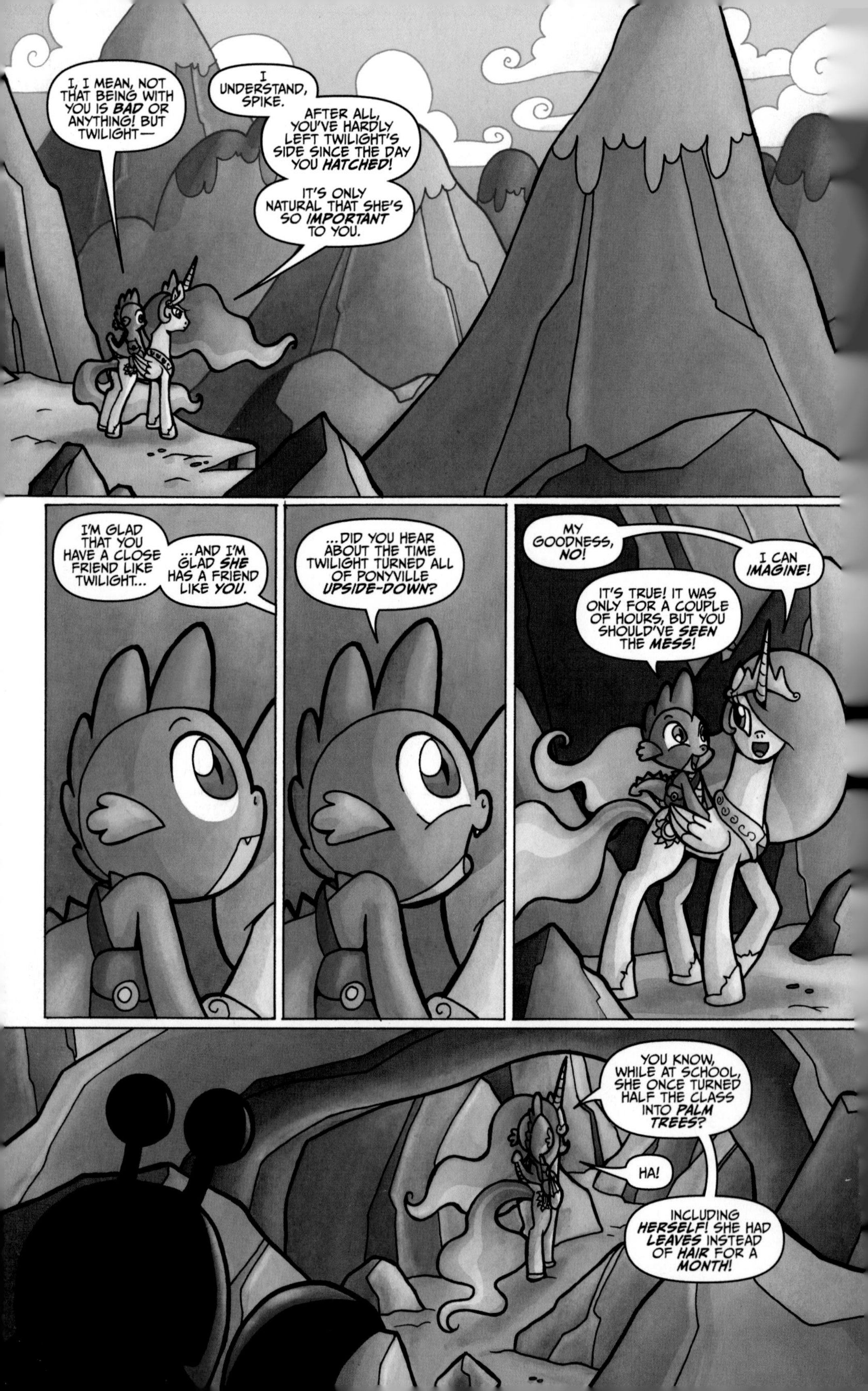
I, I MEAN, NOT THAT BEING WITH YOU IS BAD OR ANYTHING! BUT TWILIGHT—
I UNDERSTAND, SPIKE.
AFTER ALL, YOU'VE HARDLY LEFT TWILIGHT'S SIDE SINCE THE DAY YOU HATCHED!
IT'S ONLY NATURAL THAT SHE'S SO IMPORTANT TO YOU.
I'M GLAD THAT YOU HAVE A CLOSE FRIEND LIKE TWILIGHT...
...AND I'M GLAD SHE HAS A FRIEND LIKE YOU.
...DID YOU HEAR ABOUT THE TIME TWILIGHT TURNED ALL OF PONYVILLE UPSIDE-DOWN?
MY GOODNESS, NO!
IT'S TRUE! IT WAS ONLY FOR A COUPLE OF HOURS, BUT YOU SHOULD'VE SEEN THE MESS!
I CAN IMAGINE!
YOU KNOW, WHILE AT SCHOOL, SHE ONCE TURNED HALF THE CLASS INTO PALM TREES?
HA!
INCLUDING HERSELF! SHE HAD LEAVES INSTEAD OF HAIR FOR A MONTH!

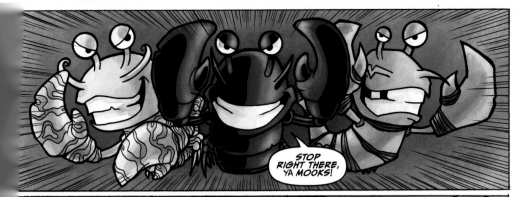

STOP RIGHT THERE, YA MOOKS!

HEH HEH HEH...

WHADDA WE GOT HERE, IGGY?

LOOKS LIKE A COUPL'A DOPES WHERE THEY SHOULDN'T BE.

YEAH.

W-W-WHO ARE YOU?

WHO ARE WE? YOU'RE THE ONES BUTTIN' IN ON OUR TURF, SCALES!

I AM PRINCESS CELESTIA, RIGHTFUL RULER OF ALL EQUESTRIA.

YOU WILL—

OOH, A PRINCESS? WELL, THEN, WE SHOULD PUT YOU UP IN OUR ROYAL SUITE!

AND SO!

DOESN'T SEEM VERY "ROYAL" TO ME.

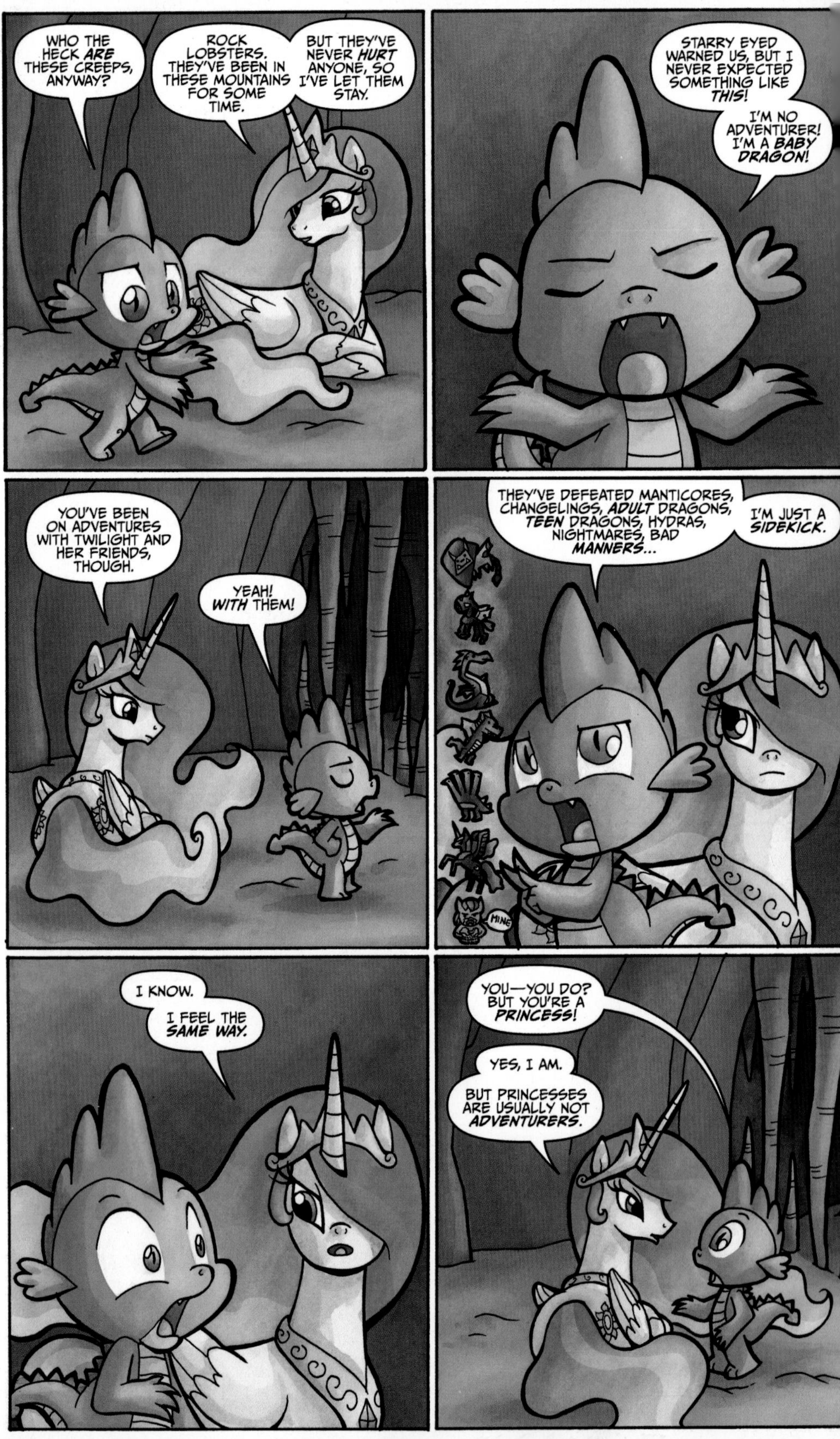
WHO THE HECK ARE THESE CREEPS, ANYWAY?
ROCK LOBSTERS. THEY'VE BEEN IN THESE MOUNTAINS FOR SOME TIME.
BUT THEY'VE NEVER HURT ANYONE, SO I'VE LET THEM STAY.
STARRY EYED WARNED US, BUT I NEVER EXPECTED SOMETHING LIKE THIS!
I'M NO ADVENTURER! I'M A BABY DRAGON!
YOU'VE BEEN ON ADVENTURES WITH TWILIGHT AND HER FRIENDS, THOUGH.
YEAH! WITH THEM!
THEY'VE DEFEATED MANTICORES, CHANGELINGS, ADULT DRAGONS, TEEN DRAGONS, HYDRAS, NIGHTMARES, BAD MANNERS...
I'M JUST A SIDEKICK.
MINE
I KNOW.
I FEEL THE SAME WAY.
YOU—YOU DO? BUT YOU'RE A PRINCESS!
YES, I AM.
BUT PRINCESSES ARE USUALLY NOT ADVENTURERS.

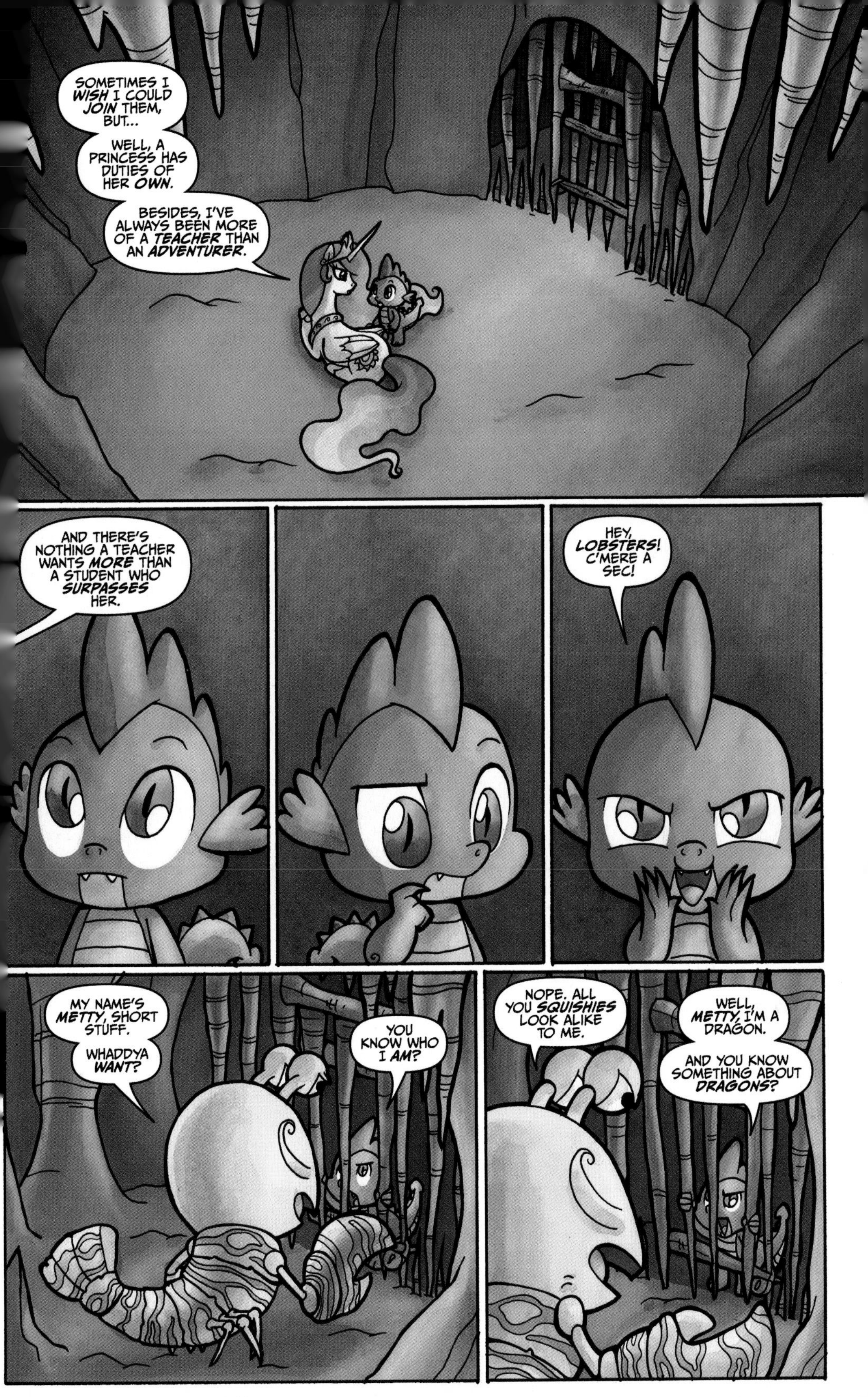
SOMETIMES I *WISH* I COULD *JOIN* THEM, BUT...
WELL, A PRINCESS HAS DUTIES OF HER *OWN*.
BESIDES, I'VE ALWAYS BEEN MORE OF A *TEACHER* THAN AN *ADVENTURER*.
AND THERE'S NOTHING A TEACHER WANTS *MORE* THAN A STUDENT WHO *SURPASSES* HER.
HEY, *LOBSTERS!* C'MERE A SEC!
MY NAME'S *METTY*, SHORT STUFF.
WHADDYA *WANT?*
YOU KNOW WHO I *AM?*
NOPE. ALL YOU *SQUISHIES* LOOK ALIKE TO ME.
WELL, *METTY*, I'M A DRAGON.
AND YOU KNOW SOMETHING ABOUT *DRAGONS?*

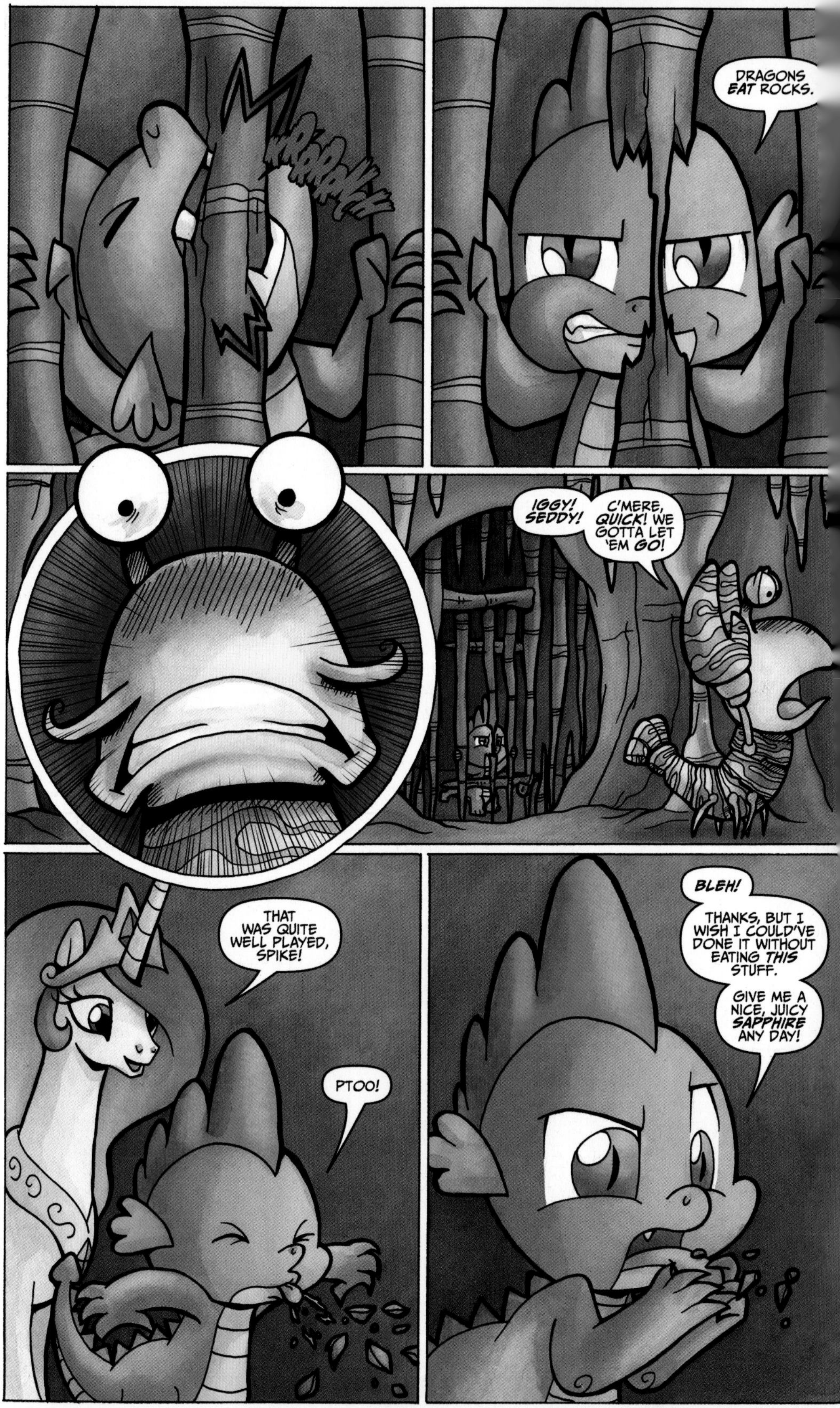
KRRRUNCH!
DRAGONS EAT ROCKS.
IGGY! SEDDY!
C'MERE, QUICK! WE GOTTA LET 'EM GO!
THAT WAS QUITE WELL PLAYED, SPIKE!
PTOO!
BLEH!
THANKS, BUT I WISH I COULD'VE DONE IT WITHOUT EATING THIS STUFF.
GIVE ME A NICE, JUICY SAPPHIRE ANY DAY!

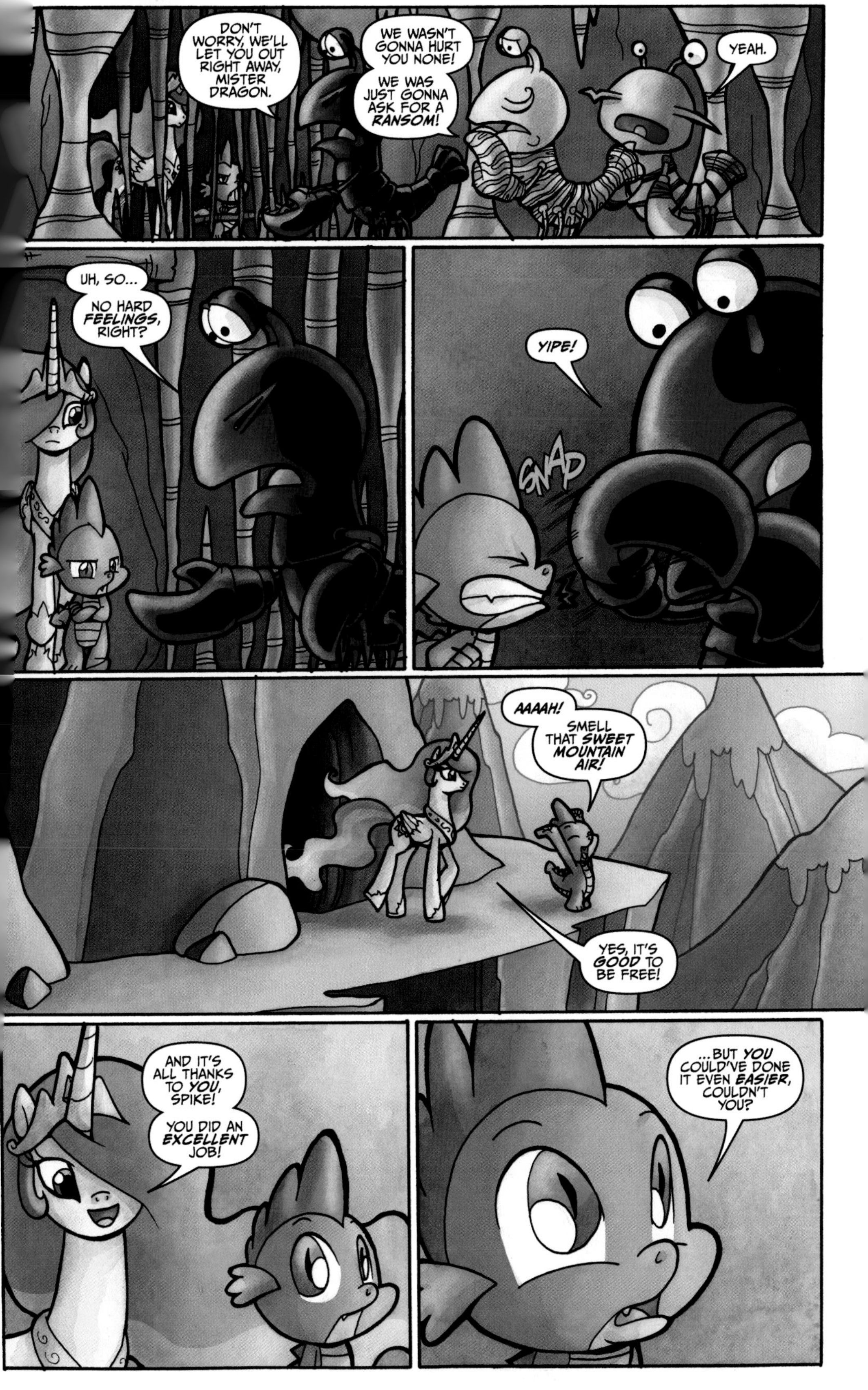

DON'T WORRY, WE'LL LET YOU OUT RIGHT AWAY, MISTER DRAGON.
WE WASN'T GONNA HURT YOU NONE!
WE WAS JUST GONNA ASK FOR A RANSOM!
YEAH.
UH, SO...
NO HARD FEELINGS, RIGHT?
YIPE!
SNAP
AAAAH!
SMELL THAT SWEET MOUNTAIN AIR!
YES, IT'S GOOD TO BE FREE!
AND IT'S ALL THANKS TO YOU, SPIKE!
YOU DID AN EXCELLENT JOB!
...BUT YOU COULD'VE DONE IT EVEN EASIER, COULDN'T YOU?

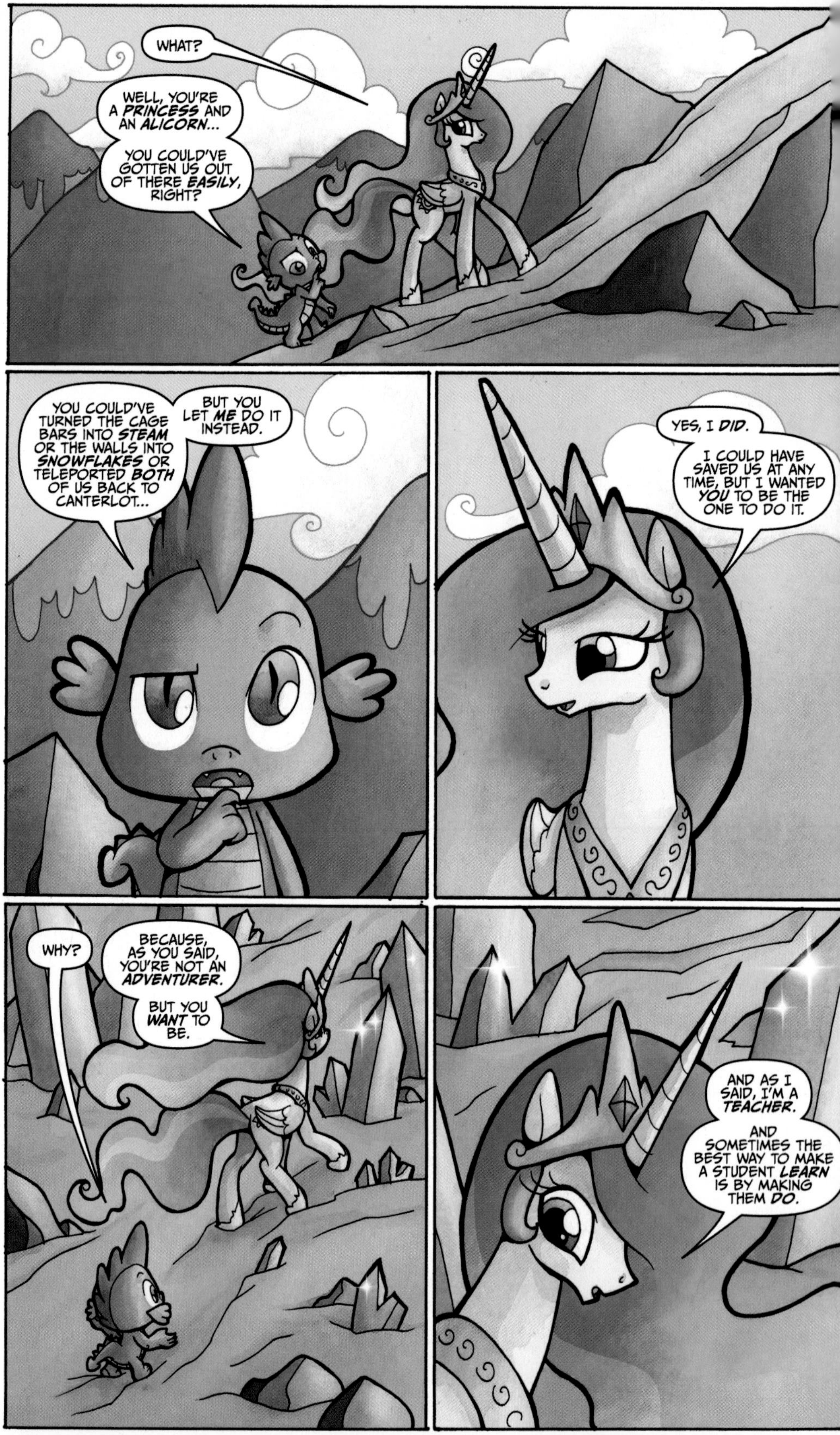
WHAT?
WELL, YOU'RE A PRINCESS AND AN ALICORN...
YOU COULD'VE GOTTEN US OUT OF THERE EASILY, RIGHT?
YOU COULD'VE TURNED THE CAGE BARS INTO STEAM OR THE WALLS INTO SNOWFLAKES OR TELEPORTED BOTH OF US BACK TO CANTERLOT...
BUT YOU LET ME DO IT INSTEAD.
YES, I DID.
I COULD HAVE SAVED US AT ANY TIME, BUT I WANTED YOU TO BE THE ONE TO DO IT.
WHY?
BECAUSE, AS YOU SAID, YOU'RE NOT AN ADVENTURER.
BUT YOU WANT TO BE.
AND AS I SAID, I'M A TEACHER.
AND SOMETIMES THE BEST WAY TO MAKE A STUDENT LEARN IS BY MAKING THEM DO.

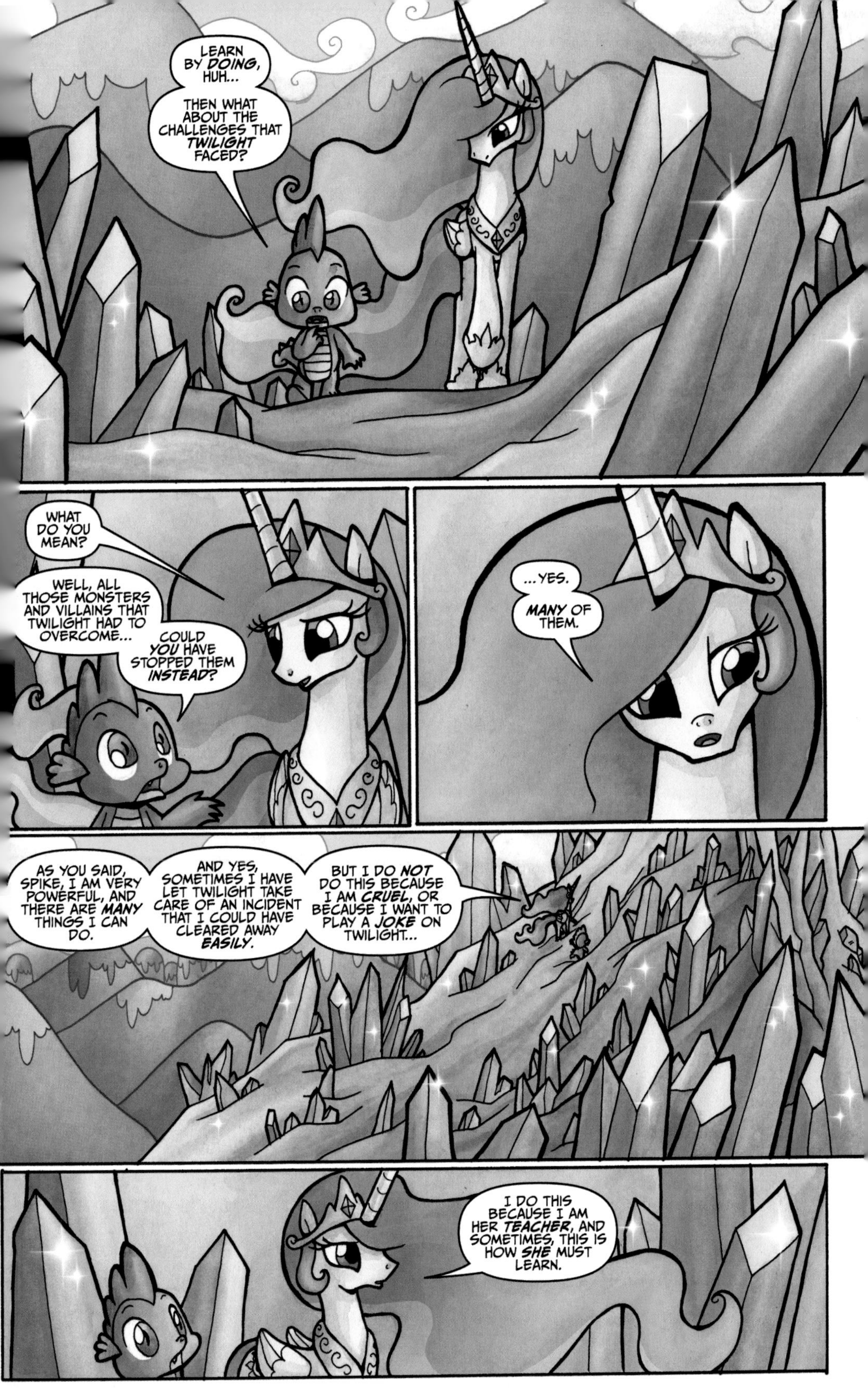
LEARN BY *DOING*, HUH...
THEN WHAT ABOUT THE CHALLENGES THAT *TWILIGHT* FACED?
WHAT DO YOU MEAN?
WELL, ALL THOSE MONSTERS AND VILLAINS THAT TWILIGHT HAD TO OVERCOME...
COULD *YOU* HAVE STOPPED THEM *INSTEAD?*
...YES.
MANY OF THEM.
AS YOU SAID, SPIKE, I AM VERY POWERFUL, AND THERE ARE *MANY* THINGS I CAN DO.
AND YES, SOMETIMES I HAVE LET TWILIGHT TAKE CARE OF AN INCIDENT THAT I COULD HAVE CLEARED AWAY *EASILY*.
BUT I DO *NOT* DO THIS BECAUSE I AM *CRUEL*, OR BECAUSE I WANT TO PLAY A *JOKE* ON TWILIGHT...
I DO THIS BECAUSE I AM HER *TEACHER*, AND SOMETIMES, THIS IS HOW *SHE* MUST LEARN.

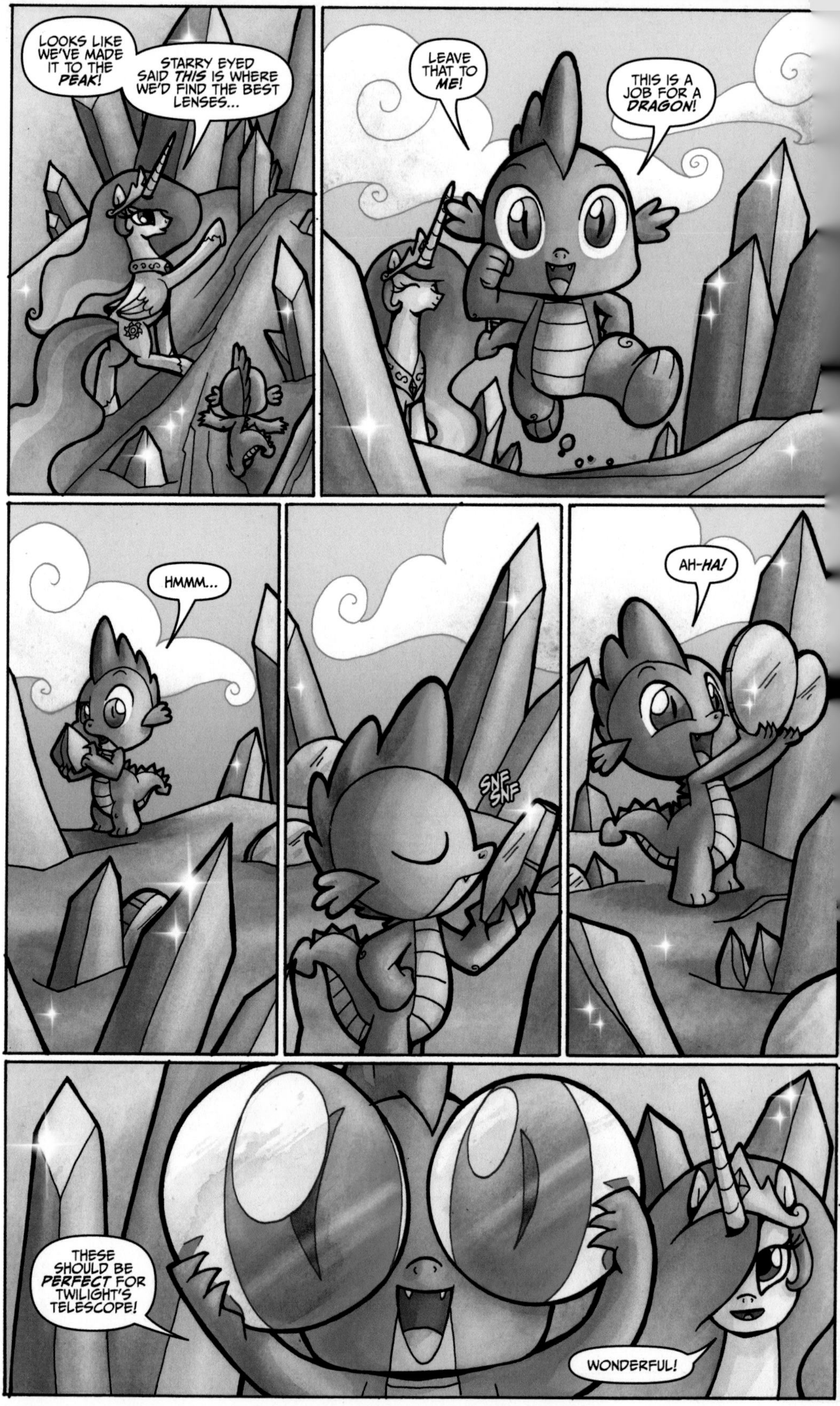
LOOKS LIKE WE'VE MADE IT TO THE PEAK!
STARRY EYED SAID THIS IS WHERE WE'D FIND THE BEST LENSES...
LEAVE THAT TO ME!
THIS IS A JOB FOR A DRAGON!
HMMM...
SNF SNF
AH-HA!
THESE SHOULD BE PERFECT FOR TWILIGHT'S TELESCOPE!
WONDERFUL!

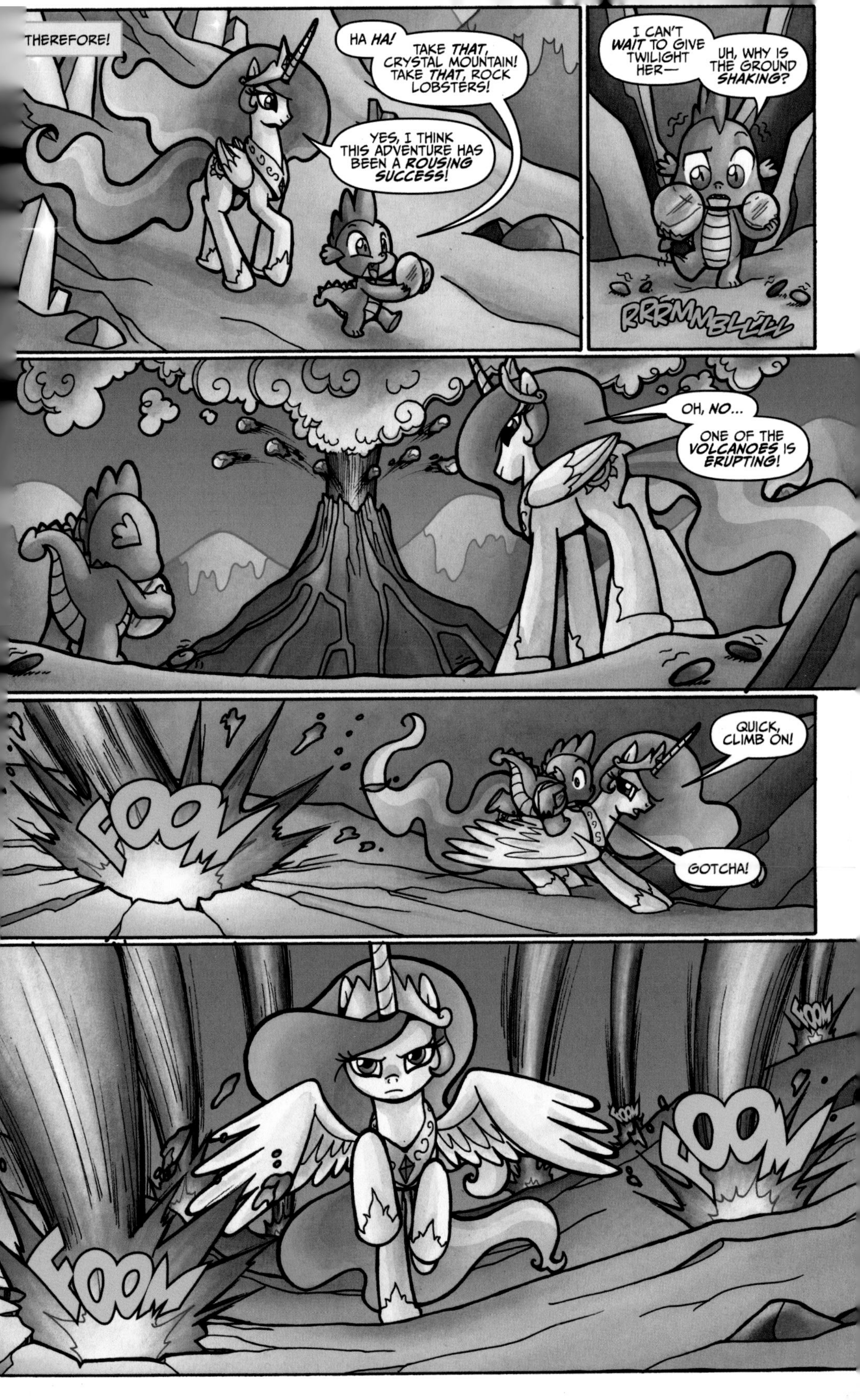
THEREFORE!
HA HA! TAKE THAT, CRYSTAL MOUNTAIN! TAKE THAT, ROCK LOBSTERS!
YES, I THINK THIS ADVENTURE HAS BEEN A ROUSING SUCCESS!
I CAN'T WAIT TO GIVE TWILIGHT HER—
UH, WHY IS THE GROUND SHAKING?
RRRMMBLLLL
OH, NO...
ONE OF THE VOLCANOES IS ERUPTING!
FOOM
QUICK, CLIMB ON!
GOTCHA!
FOOM
FOOM
FOOM
FOOM

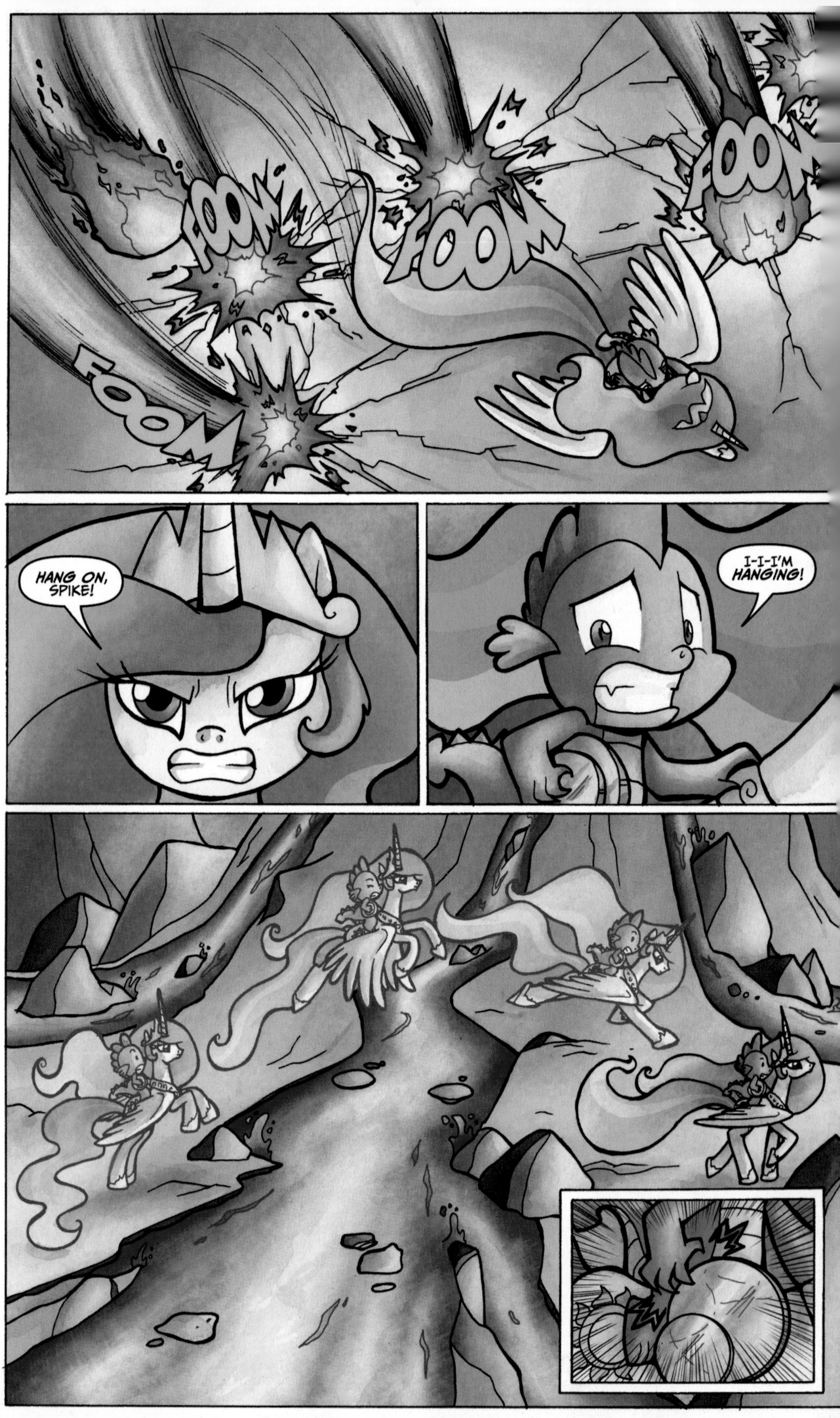
FOOM
FOOM
FOOM
FOOM
HANG ON, SPIKE!
I-I-I'M HANGING!

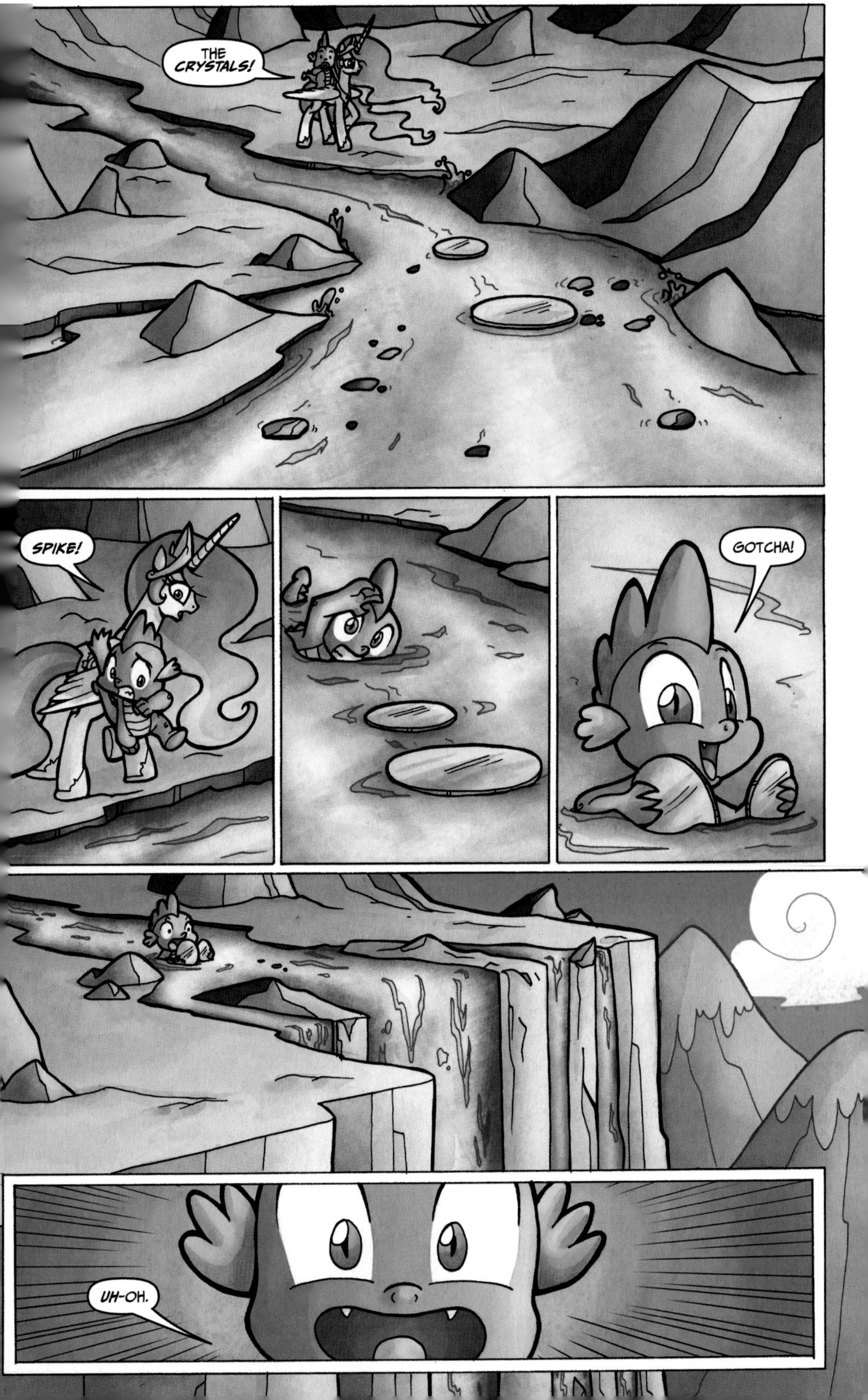
THE CRYSTALS!
SPIKE!
GOTCHA!
UH-OH.

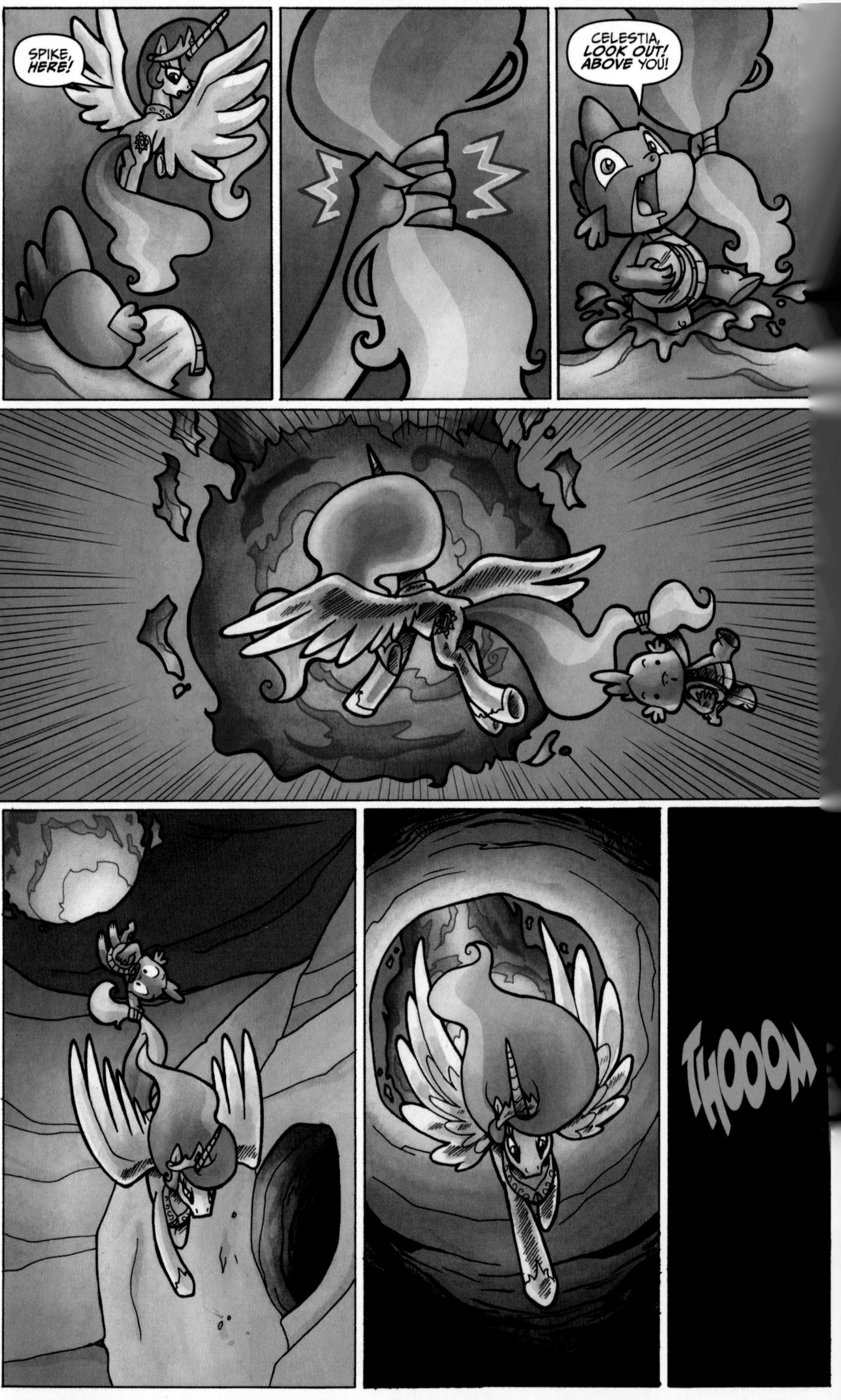
SPIKE, HERE!
CELESTIA, LOOK OUT! ABOVE YOU!
THOOOM

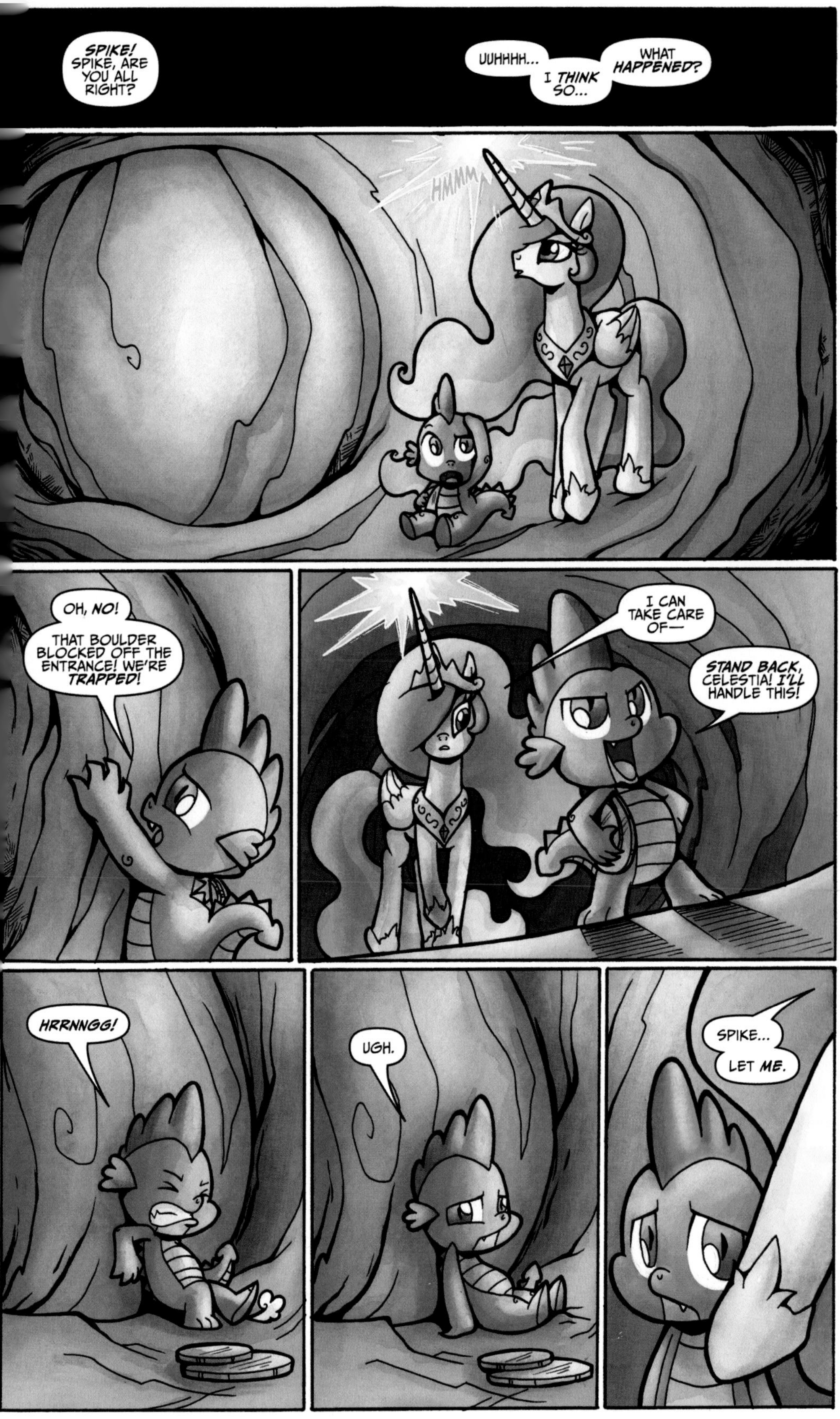
SPIKE! SPIKE, ARE YOU ALL RIGHT?
UUHHHH...
I THINK SO...
WHAT HAPPENED?
HMMM
OH, NO!
THAT BOULDER BLOCKED OFF THE ENTRANCE! WE'RE TRAPPED!
I CAN TAKE CARE OF—
STAND BACK, CELESTIA! I'LL HANDLE THIS!
HRRNNGG!
UGH.
SPIKE...
LET ME.

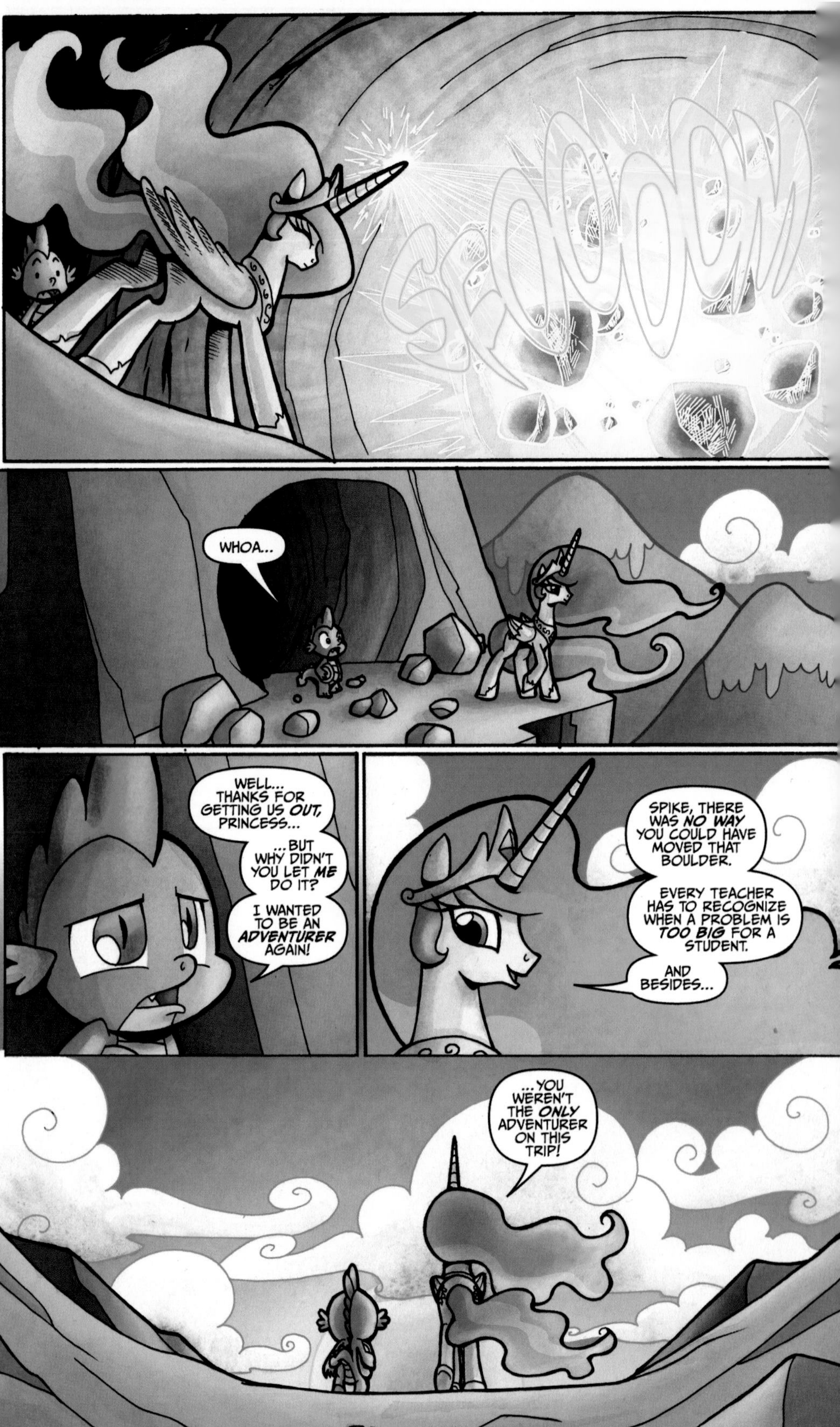
SKOOOOM
WHOA...
WELL... THANKS FOR GETTING US OUT, PRINCESS...
...BUT WHY DIDN'T YOU LET ME DO IT?
I WANTED TO BE AN ADVENTURER AGAIN!
SPIKE, THERE WAS NO WAY YOU COULD HAVE MOVED THAT BOULDER.
EVERY TEACHER HAS TO RECOGNIZE WHEN A PROBLEM IS TOO BIG FOR A STUDENT.
AND BESIDES...
...YOU WEREN'T THE ONLY ADVENTURER ON THIS TRIP!

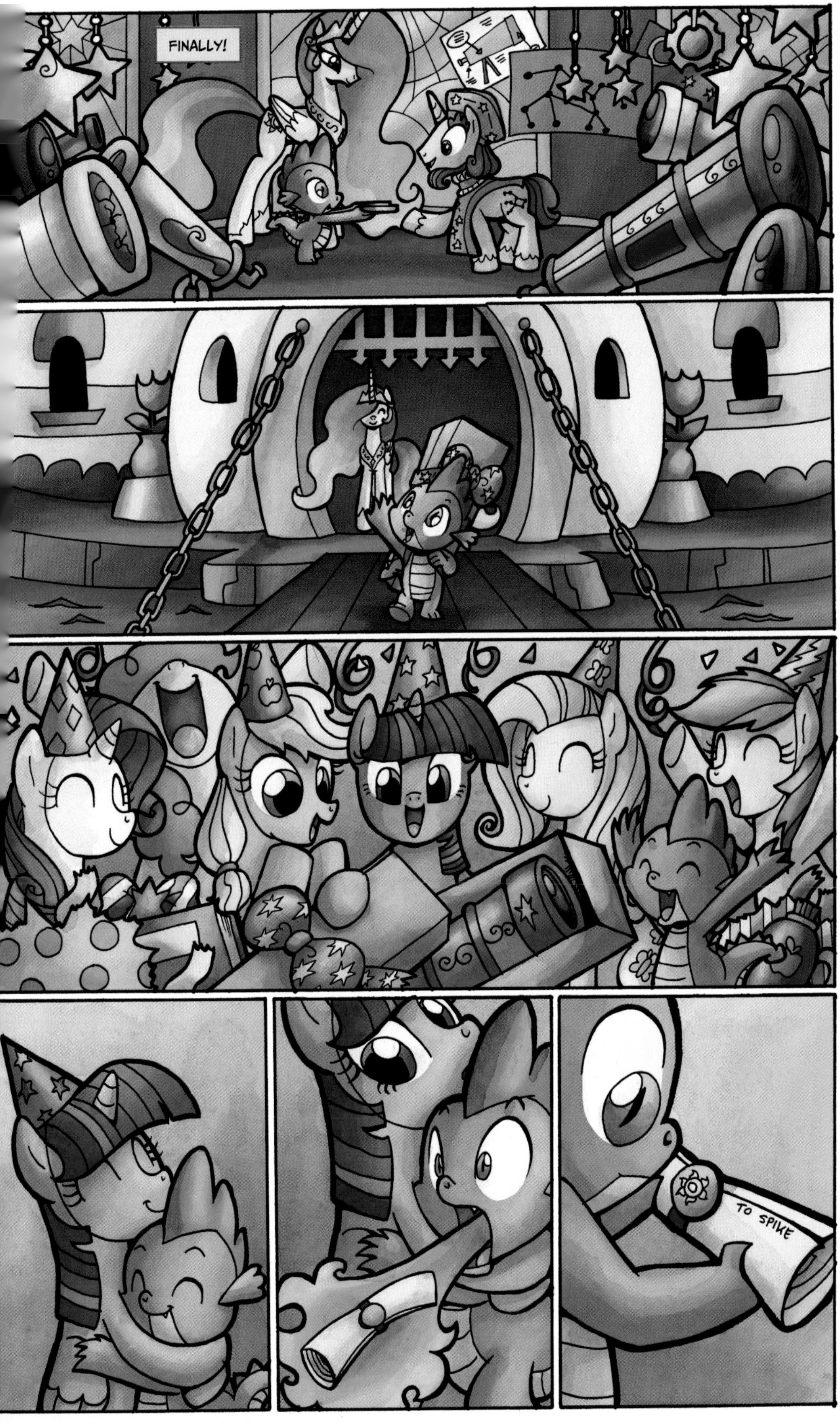
FINALLY!
TO SPIKE

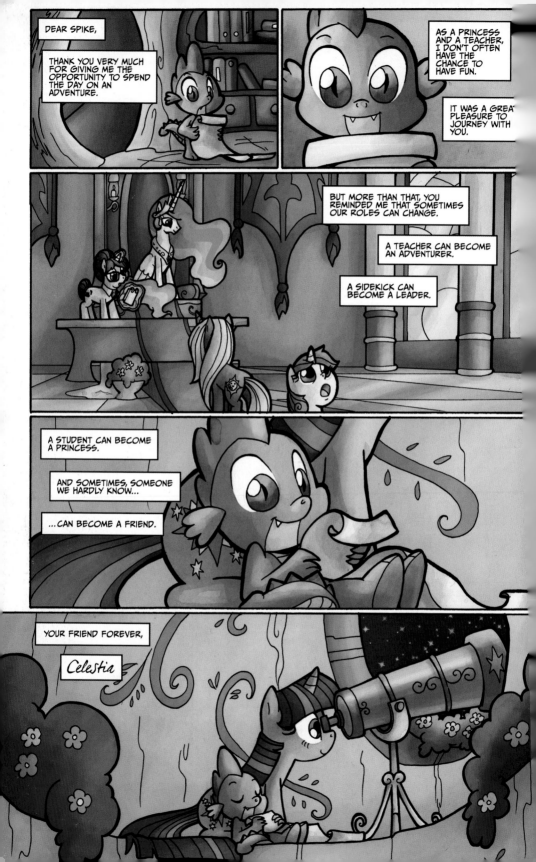

DEAR SPIKE,

THANK YOU VERY MUCH FOR GIVING ME THE OPPORTUNITY TO SPEND THE DAY ON AN ADVENTURE.

AS A PRINCESS AND A TEACHER, I DON'T OFTEN HAVE THE CHANCE TO HAVE FUN.

IT WAS A GREAT PLEASURE TO JOURNEY WITH YOU.

BUT MORE THAN THAT, YOU REMINDED ME THAT SOMETIMES OUR ROLES CAN CHANGE.

A TEACHER CAN BECOME AN ADVENTURER.

A SIDEKICK CAN BECOME A LEADER.

A STUDENT CAN BECOME A PRINCESS.

AND SOMETIMES, SOMEONE WE HARDLY KNOW...

...CAN BECOME A FRIEND.

YOUR FRIEND FOREVER,

Celestia

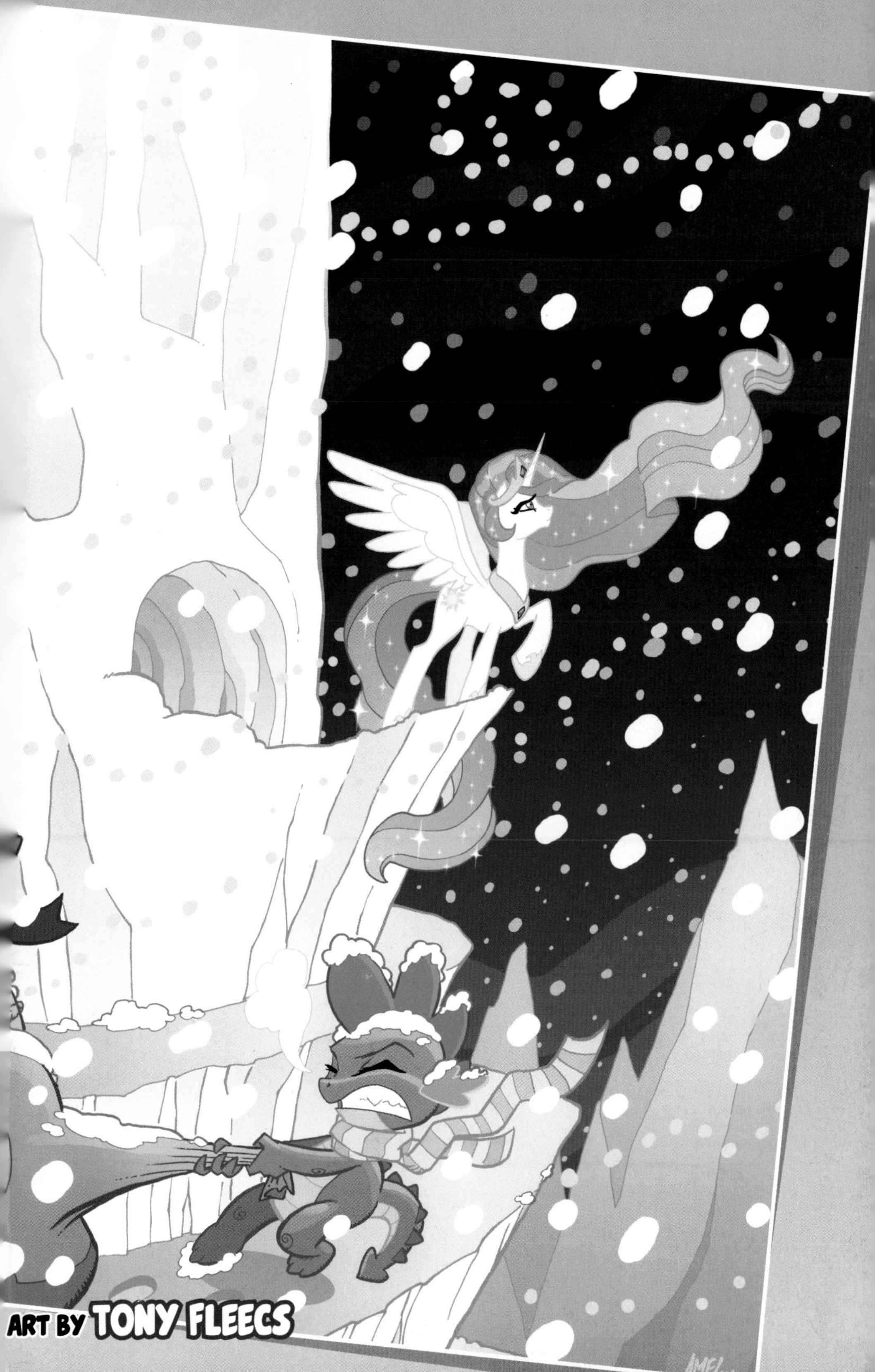
ART BY TONY FLEECS

These collections on sale now!

My Little Pony: Friendship Is Magic, Vol. 1
ISBN: 978-1-61377-605-6

My Little Pony: Pony Tales, Vol. 1
ISBN: 978-1-61377-740-4

My Little Pony: The Magic Begins
ISBN: 978-1-61377-754-1

Licensed By:

IDW
Hasbro

www.idwpublishing.com
Hasbro and its logo, MY LITTLE PONY, and all related characters are trademarks
of Hasbro and are used with permission. © 2014 Hasbro. All Rights Reserved.

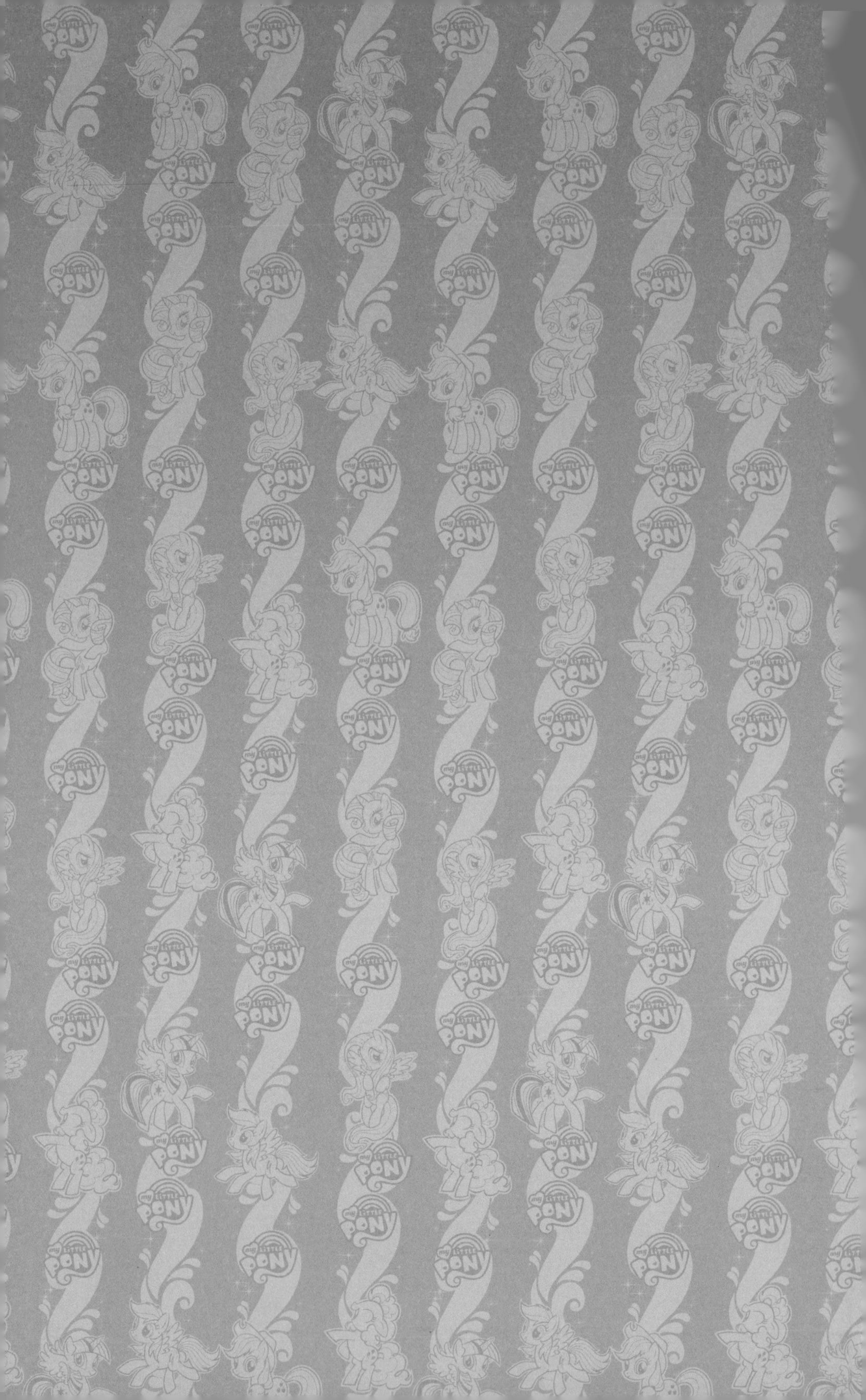